CULDESAC

Also by Robert Repino

Mort(e)

D'Arc

CULDESAC

A NOVELLA FROM THE WAR WITH NO NAME
BY ROBERT REPINO

SOHO

Published by
Soho Press, Inc.
853 Broadway
New York, NY 10003

Library of Congress Cataloging-in-Publication Data
is available upon request.

ISBN 978-1-61695-819-0
eISBN 978-1-61695-820-6

Interior design by Janine Agro, Soho Press, Inc.

Printed in the United States of America

10 9 8 7 6 5 4 3 2 1

For d.f. and m.p.

INTRODUCTION

THE HUMANS NEVER saw it coming. For thousands of years, the Colony studied their weaknesses, bred an army of soldiers, and planned the exact moment to strike. From her underground lair, the Queen of the ants learned what made the humans afraid. She knew how to break them. And in doing so, she would bring about a new order, a world cleansed of humanity, peaceful and free.

The war with no name began quietly, with a series of distractions. Then the second wave hit: Alpha soldiers, giant ants rising from the earth to devour any human that crossed their path. Governments collapsed in weeks. Entire continents were overrun.

And then, the third wave. Using a mysterious technology, the Queen transformed the surface animals into intelligent beings. A gift that no god could ever bestow upon them. Suddenly, farm animals, ferals, and pets could think and speak. Their bodies changed, allowing them to walk on their hind legs and use their hands like a human. And so a new front in the war opened, pitting slave against master—a final reckoning for the sins of humanity. Fighting for the Queen, the animals would avenge the cruelties inflicted on them and build a new future.

But the humans were stubborn. Unwilling to surrender, they

developed a weapon of last resort: the EMSAH Syndrome, a virus with the potential to destroy all life on earth. If the humans could not rule, then no one would.

The bobcat Culdesac has sworn his life to the new order. Favored by the Queen for his bravery and ruthlessness, he leads the Red Sphinx, an elite unit fighting a guerilla war deep in human territory. At his side is Mort(e), his second in command, chosen by the Queen herself to one day defeat the EMSAH scourge. But time is running out. For every day the humans live, the revolution hangs in the balance, and only the cruel, the mad, and the savage will see the war through to final victory.

CHAPTER ONE
BECAUSE THE RABBIT

THE MAN FLED into the forest with a deep wound torn into his hip that left red droplets in the dirt. Though he ran at first—ran for his life with no regard to where he was going—his gait slowed to a limp after a few miles. His right foot pressed boot prints in the soft mud, revealing him to wear a size nine, or even an eight. A small man, probably driven and stubborn, eager to fight over nothing, like so many other humans his height. His left footprint revealed his dire situation. With the shoe missing, the prints left the formless shape of a damp sock. After four miles of slogging through the hills, a stick or a sharp stone must have punctured the skin, for each print included a diamond-shaped red mark on the ball of the foot, the size of a quarter. The first time Culdesac saw it, he dropped to his stomach and sniffed the patch of glistening crimson. He stuck out his tongue and licked it, enough to pull in the taste of the earth, along with the distinct iron of the blood. He let it sit in his mouth until the fragrance wafted out of his nose with each exhale.

Oh, Culdesac missed the hunt.

Like a good bobcat, he grew up stalking prey in the wilderness. In those days—when he was a mere animal, doomed to die of starvation once he grew too old—Culdesac learned that no prey could cover its tracks forever. Even the cleverest among them—the rabbits, the squirrels—would make a mistake, for no one could tread through the forest without altering it. The forest could hide a person as well as give them away.

This human was definitely clever. After some time, he must have tied a bandage to his injured foot, for the precious red diamonds vanished. Soon after, Culdesac noticed circular indentations, most likely from a cane the human fashioned from a tree branch. The man used the cane to climb the hill, to get to rockier terrain where tracking would rely more on instinct rather than smell. Then again, the mountains provided less cover, and the human moved more slowly by the hour. This path he chose may have provided the best possibility of escape, but it was a gamble, the kind expected of a man bleeding to death.

After a mile, the trail forked in two directions. One path led higher into the rocky area of the hills, the other dropped into the forest. Culdesac imagined the choice before the weary human. Climb the mountain and risk further exhaustion, or take the easier route, where he would continue to leave marks in the dirt, broken twigs, disturbed patches of grass. The forest trail eventually led to farmlands, overgrown and abandoned, the crops choking each other out and congealing into brown mush. According to the latest reports from the Colony, a human army waited nearby, most likely under the command of General Fitzpatrick. Perhaps the human expected to make it all that way—a pure fantasy, judging from his condition.

A scent wafted along, tickling Culdesac's nose. He crouched and sniffed again. The odor came from the forest. The bobcat smiled before bounding down the trail. The smell grew stronger. Definitely urine, very acidic, sticking to the insides of his nostrils. The human finally slipped up and relieved himself out in the open, marking his territory. Perhaps he knew that this would be the last time he would feel the simple pleasure of an empty bladder. When the smell grew even more pungent, Culdesac wondered if the man pissed himself, either out of fear or because he lost control of his functions in his weakened state. Maybe Culdesac would discover his prey slumped against a tree, dead, one last cigarette still smoking in his petrified lips.

At an elbow in the trail, the stink became unbearable. Culdesac spun around, checking behind trees, searching for indentations in the mud. Nothing. He dropped to all fours and sniffed every inch until he came across a canteen wedged between two large rocks. He lifted it from its hiding place and recoiled from the smell inside. Culdesac turned to the hilltop behind him, where the sun prepared to sink behind the ridge.

Very clever, he thought.

The man must have pissed in the canteen, screwed the cap on loosely, and then tossed it from the hilltop. It hit the ground and burst open, releasing its contents. The molecules found their way to Culdesac's sensitive nose, leading him in the wrong direction. The humans learned to exploit the animals' sense of smell far too late to win the war, a fact that failed to make Culdesac feel any better.

The bobcat slammed the canteen on the dirt and ran back the way he came, not caring how much noise he made. Only when he returned to the fork in the trail did he try to calculate the time lost. If he wanted to kill this man, it would take him at least another day, maybe more. Culdesac's troops waited for him at the town he left behind, with orders to secure the area. The envoy from the Colony would arrive in a couple of days to deliver the latest report on the human army. Culdesac had time. And besides, after all the trouble this man caused, Culdesac needed to bring back his head.

On the ridge, the trees gave way to smaller shrubs, and the stony scalp of the mountain broke through the dirt. The scent trail went completely blank, forcing him to crawl with his nose to the ground. He was losing time, but the human left him little choice. He needed only a small hint of where the man went in order to break into a run. If his claws scraping on the rock gave away his position, so be it. Let the human spend his last moments knowing that death could find him even in this peaceful place.

The stink of human sweat popped up again near a thatch of bushes growing stubbornly among the stones. The wind bent them over, forcing them to grow at an angle. Stashed beneath the leaves was a white box, a first aid kit. Both sides in the war hid supplies in the woods for retrieval in situations like this, and the human surely did not come across it by accident. Culdesac noticed gauze, tweezers, thread for stitches, a wrapper for a protein bar, an empty bottle of antibiotics. This tiny supply depot may have even included a fresh pair of boots. The human patched himself together and left these items, maybe to show Culdesac that the game had changed, and that he was now hunting a human who found a way to survive even on the run from death. The man may have enjoyed a brief spell of euphoria as he sealed the wound, filled his belly, gazed out to the countryside dreaming of some nebulous future when this madness would fall behind him. It must have been nice.

Ah, but this human did not know the bobcat who chased him. Culdesac was no mere conscript in the war with no name. He fought it his entire life, long before the Queen uplifted him, changing him from an animal into something more. He knew this forest, having explored it as a cub many summers before. He learned these trails precisely because of what the humans did to his people before the uprising. In those days, the habitats shrank every year, hemmed in by new roads, construction projects, hunters prowling in their obscene orange vests. Culdesac stalked his territory with his mother and brother, always fearful of the unnatural noises that grew louder in the distance, the sound of humans uprooting the forest, severing trees at the root, carving out new paths with their war machines. At first, the arrival of the humans provided a boon to the predators, as it forced the deer to cross through bobcat territory. But this lasted only a season, and soon the bobcats took to fighting one another over the last scraps of wilderness left.

He and his brother did not have names. Culdesac knew his brother by scent, and by the growling noise his mother made when she called him. When something dangerous approached, his mother let out two quick grunts: *mer-mer*. At night, when they ate from a carcass, Culdesac's brother would sometimes lick the blood from his mother's face and paws. In those moments, she would say his name more gently, both a salutation and a thank-you. Years later, after the Change gave Culdesac the ability to speak, he thought of his brother as Murmur. A fitting name for a powerful bobcat who rarely needed to speak.

One morning, Culdesac woke in his hovel to the sound of his brother baying in the early morning light. When he crawled out, he sensed an absence, an emptiness, and knew then why his brother cried. Their mother had gone missing in the night. Perhaps she abandoned them, having gone so many days without eating in order to make sure they were fed. Or maybe someone killed her, or some other male chose her for his own clan. Culdesac would never know, and the forest would never tell.

A few weeks later, while slinking along a well-worn path, a loud clap from somewhere far off made Culdesac jump. Murmur fell to his side with a red wound bubbling on his ribs. Culdesac pawed at him, begging him to get up. But footsteps, and the stink of some unknown animal, sent him running. He took cover in the bushes while a pack of humans surrounded his brother. Each of the men wore clothes that mimicked the surrounding foliage. For the next two hours, Culdesac watched as the humans cut the young bobcat apart. They severed the tail and passed it among themselves. They lopped off the paws before starting on the coat. It took two of the humans to tear the skin from the muscle. Doing so released a horrible scent, a combination of blood and the cloying pheromone of the females with whom Culdesac had mated. He swore that his brother was still breathing. The head came off last, a tedious process that required hacking and sawing. When he became sentient, Culdesac discovered similar animal trophies in the homes that the humans abandoned in the war. He imagined one day coming across a house where his brother's head would be mounted above the fireplace, the eyes replaced with glass marbles, the mouth propped open, the fangs polished white. He would remove Murmur's head and replace it with the human's—after repeating the same process he witnessed here.

When the humans left, Culdesac visited what remained of his brother, a mere pile of flesh with the head and tail removed, the bones exposed, the entrails cast aside and swarmed by flies. From then on, Culdesac was on his own.

So he knew this forest. And he knew where the human was going.

At the foot of the mountain, the river was wide, too wide for a weakened, shivering human with fresh stitches. But backtracking along the riverbed would bring him to a dead tree that lay across the river. Culdesac traversed it many times in his younger days. He did not have a name for it then, though the rough surface of the tree bark made him think of it as a cat's tongue stretching across the river. In his uplifted state, when he could think abstractly and use words, he could give it a name, the way the humans did with all of this land that they thought they owned. He would call it The Lick, and when he returned to the town with this human's skull, he would write the new name on a map of the area. It made him smile. Soon all of this would be reclaimed, every last body of water, every last mountain. Not a trace of the human age would remain.

Culdesac made it to the river by nightfall. Sure enough, the desiccated log carried a hint of rubber boots and sweat. A fresh gash in the rotting bark suggested that the man slipped and tore off a piece. If the human found the need to urinate again, he probably did his business in the river to hide both the sound and the smell. But it was too late for that. He could hide no longer. He could only run, and even that would merely delay the inevitable. Satisfied, Culdesac pulled a bottle of water from his backpack and refilled it in the river. He smiled again, knowing that the human could drink the water here only by boiling it, a tedious method that would only waste time, give away his position. The human would quench his thirst while death gained on him.

Culdesac made his way to the other side of the valley before stopping to rest. In his dreamless sleep, he nevertheless could hear his brother crying out, his voice going dead amidst the trees.

A few kilometers from the river, with the sun rising, Culdesac slowed as the scent grew stronger, and the tracks and markings seemed fresher. At this time of day, imperfections in the terrain cast longer shadows. Soon, Culdesac found a broken twig above an uneven patch of grass, still moist to the touch. A muddy boot print on a boulder confirmed that the man traveled in new foot-wear. And soon, Culdesac could smell food: a granola bar with peanut butter.

On all fours, Culdesac crept through the trees, trying to blend in. He heard the human breathing, the voice low to the ground. A pair of shoes scuffed against the gravel, then stopped. Culdesac spotted him first. Crouched against a tree, about twenty paces away, the man tried to hold his breath as he looked around. Between a thatch of unkempt hair and a filthy beard, two hazel eyes darted about. His machine gun sat propped against the trunk. As Culdesac expected, the man wore the same camouflaged outfit that the hunters wore when they skinned his brother alive. Culdesac remained still, his charcoal ears and flecked fur indistinguishable amidst the tree branches. When their eyes met, the man still needed some time to get a fix on the demon staring at him through the bush. Culdesac bolted. The branches and leaves brushed his face as he ran. His field of vision shrank to a tunnel, with the hapless man struggling to his feet to get away. As the human tried to barrel roll toward the gun, Culdesac lunged and raked his claw across the man's ribs and down his waist. Hot blood burst from the three jagged lines cut into the man's flesh. Grunting, the man kicked Culdesac in the face and snatched the weapon. When he turned and fired, Culdesac slipped behind a tree. The bullets tore through the foliage and ripped out chunks of earth. The noise echoed all the way through the valley. When he stopped, a strange silence descended on the forest.

The man rolled on to his stomach and crawled along a trail that led to a clearing. Culdesac followed, taking cover each time he moved in case the man summoned the energy to take another shot. But this was the end. Culdesac could smell it in the blood. He could hear it in the fluid that rattled in the man's ribs.

Exhausted, the human propped himself on a log that had fallen across the clearing, his hand sealed to the bloody wound. The stitching from the night before hung in tatters, the twine sticking out from the shredded skin. The bobcat rose to his hind legs, an ability that the humans seemed to fear even more than the animals' intelligence. There was something about the creatures rising from their savage state that showed the humans that their reign of terror was over, and new masters would have dominion over the earth.

The man kept his cool, though he could not hide the pain from his wound. His lips parted to reveal gritted teeth, painted red with blood. With a shaky hand, he attempted to raise the barrel of his gun. In a blur, Culdesac snatched it away from him. The man did not even have time to blink.

"Gaw 'head and do it," the man said.

Culdesac tossed the gun aside and put his fingers to his lips. "Shhhhh." He opened his pack and pulled out a metal flask, filled with whiskey. A gift from the company medic, a housecat named Socks who insisted on renaming himself Tiberius. Culdesac unscrewed the cap and offered the flask to the human.

"For the pain," the bobcat said.

The man hesitated. He then reached out his blood-soaked hand and took the flask. He sniffed it, raised an eyebrow, and took a long pull. He pressed his thumb to his mouth to hold in a cough. Then he nodded. "It's good."

"Take as much as you need."

Culdesac sat in front of the man and watched as he took a few more sips. The human's gristly Adam's apple bobbed with each swallow. By the third or fourth drink, the eyelids fluttered. On an empty stomach, the whiskey acted quickly. The human probably thought of a time before the war, when he could drink this firewater and doze off in front of a television or on a porch swing in the summer.

"What now?" the man asked.

"Do you really want to know?"

The human shrugged.

"I will let you go to sleep. Then I will cook you and eat you. I have developed a taste for barbecued flesh."

The human rolled his eyes and took his longest sip so far.

"Then I have to bring your head back to the town," Culdesac continued. "In the firefight, you killed one of my top lieutenants. A cat named Luna. Even though we won the battle, I owed it to her to find you."

"I'm honored," the man said.

Culdesac paused. "Why did you attack? We secured the town. We had the high ground, the shooting lines, a base of operations. It was suicide."

"We got one o' you, didn't we?"

"One," Culdesac said. "Was it worth it?"

"I guess I won't know. But we did slow you down. Let you know this won't be an easy war for ya. None of 'em are easy."

Some real wisdom from a human, Culdesac thought. Impressive. This man would not tell him the real reason his unit attacked, which left Culdesac with the theory that they simply ran out of supplies and needed to raid the town. A plausible if unsatisfying possibility.

"I told my soldiers to take some time off," Culdesac said bitterly. "Before you came. With the humans pushed back, I thought we could relax." Culdesac remembered it perfectly: Tiberius leading the cats in drinking games, Jomo and Cromwell performing feats of strength, Bentley insisting that no one disturb him while he slept, Brutal trying to mate with Sugar for the eighth or ninth time, Sugar dropping him with a punch to the face. And then, cutting through the revelry, a gunshot, followed by shouting as the sentries yelled for help. And then the blur of a firefight began, turning these uplifted creatures into animals once more, beasts driven by instinct and fighting for survival.

"I wish *you* took some time off," the man said.

"I did. This is how I relax."

The man tried to laugh, but could only expel a few puffs of

air. By then, his face had gone white, and a drop of blood-tinged saliva hung precariously from his bottom lip.

"Don't none of this bother you?" the man said.

Culdesac pictured his brother's mangled corpse again. "Did you ever ask yourself that same question?" he asked. "The method I used to hunt you—following you for days until you grew exhausted—that is exactly how your people learned to do it. That is how you evolved. It helped your brains to grow. It allowed you to think creatively. Abstractly. All your accomplishments come from violence, not inspiration. Not love. Not God."

"I don't wanna debate," the man said. "I just wanna know: Did the Queen give you a conscience? She give you...empathy? There were some animals who had it before the Change. Looks like she took it away."

"The Queen only gave. She never took."

"That's how it starts with dictators. But you'll see. You'll see."

"*You* won't."

Culdesac told the man to enjoy the rest of the whiskey while he built a fire. As the bobcat gathered sticks and dug out a pit, the human watched helplessly, his jaw propped on his shoulder as he faded out. The blood pooled at the man's side, sticky and bright red against the soil. Haltingly, with labored breaths, the man began a story he once heard, a legend of how bobcats got their spots. A hungry bobcat once chased a rabbit up a tree. The rabbit, being the smarter of the two, talked the bobcat into building a fire so he could cook his dinner. But after the bobcat lit the flame, a great wind came along and blew the embers onto his coat, singeing the fur and sending the animal running into the forest.

"That's how," the man stammered, "that's how you got. Your spots. Because the rabbit..."

The flask dropped the ground, letting out a hollow *thunk*. The man slumped over, his dead eyes twinkling. Culdesac walked over and picked up the flask. He toasted the deceased, both the human and Luna, and took a swig. The whiskey mixed with blood tasted lovely. And now the alcohol would flavor the man's flesh while he cooked on the spit, a just reward for Culdesac's hard work.

CHAPTER TWO
MILTON

HIS BELLY FULL, Culdesac carried the freshly boiled skull in his backpack, along with the machine gun that the man used to kill Luna. After months of eating protein rations supplied by the Colony, the flavor of whiskey-marinated human meat left a tangy, satisfying aftertaste. Culdesac figured that he would one day coin a term for cooked human flesh, the same way that humans came up with names for animal meat. It would have to be an entirely new word to separate the people from the sustenance that their flesh provided. That must have been the reason the humans used words like bacon, pork, mutton: to remove any trace of personhood from the protein that they shoveled into their faces.

He raised this issue with his soldiers once, over a roaring fire in which two downed pilots turned on spits, their skin crackling. Tiberius wanted to use an existing word and change it slightly. "Let's call it *hork*," he said, hiccupping. Biko insisted on the word *mank*, though he was unable to explain what that even meant. Someone else shouted *shank*, a term that quickly gained a large following, though this devolved into a discussion about giving names to different parts of the body, the way humans did with cows. As the debate grew more heated, one of the carcasses fell into the flames, and Uzi—Culdesac's personal bodyguard—burned herself trying to salvage it. The cat Bicker, who grew up in a garbage dump, gamely agreed to eat the parts that were charred beyond recognition. Culdesac thanked them both by giving them an extra six-pack of beer.

Culdesac could not linger in the memory too long. There was work to do when he returned. Barring any setbacks, he would arrive in time to meet the envoy from the Colony, who would provide the latest orders for the Red Sphinx. He expected that his unit would continue pushing west toward the human front. There, they would help the regular army— infiltrating the enemy camps, sabotaging their equipment, assassinating some officers. The usual.

At the same time, Culdesac needed to check the morale of his unit—without appearing to do so. The Red Sphinx could scavenge for a few days, but grew bored quickly. They were assassins, not a standing army meant to occupy a pacified area. Culdesac's new Number One, the cat named Mort(e), was left in charge for the first time since replacing Luna. A few of the soldiers—especially the ones still loyal to Luna—must have considered the possibility that she would still be alive were it not for Culdesac demoting her so quickly. Culdesac could not yet tell any of them the truth: the Queen herself chose Mort(e) to rise through the ranks. She had big plans for him, and Culdesac would have to rely on the housecat to fulfill his promise and keep everyone in line.

The town itself did not make things any easier. Once called Milton, the little hamlet resembled so many other deserted places Culdesac encountered, with a lonely highway ramp leading onto a main street consisting of gas stations, bars, a church, a school, a strip mall. Several rows of houses cut into the forest beyond. An old factory, abandoned long before the war, sat rotting near the train tracks, its boarded windows covered with graffiti, a black hole of decay that sucked in the surrounding buildings. A decades-old housing project quarantined the poor from the rest of the community. Several monuments to the town's history stood rusting in the more prosperous neighborhood, including a war memorial and a few plaques commemorating houses that were used for both the Underground Railroad and for bootlegging.

Milton thus held little strategic value, and yet the humans barricaded themselves in the fire station all the same, fighting to the last man. Their presence suggested that a larger offensive was coming, and a dangerous one at that. The humans grew more desperate, especially with the fall of their provisional government in the Rockies. If they were going to stem the tide of the uprising, they would have to attack, to retake the land one worthless town at a time. More of Culdesac's soldiers would die. Some might even run away. Dark days lay ahead. Luckily, his species could see at night.

Culdesac did not reach the outskirts of Milton until the predawn hours of the following morning. With the electricity long since shut down, the civilians took to lighting torches in the town square for light. There, the Red Sphinx formed a defensive perimeter, a safe zone taking up a few residential blocks. Any civilian who wanted to stay would have to remain inside of it. They could go foraging only with permission, and everyone—even those who wanted to move along—would have to be tested for EMSAH, the bioweapon deployed by the humans. By then, the animals of Milton knew the stories of quarantined sectors, occupied by Colonial Alpha soldiers and destroyed overnight. Culdesac needed to mention it only once to keep the people in line.

Outside of the safe zone, the darkness clung to the houses. The nocturnal residents—rats and raccoons—went about their business of collecting food from the nearby forest and storing it in the abandoned buildings. They could still get by on acorns and such. A few of them recognized Culdesac as he walked through. One of them, a wispy raccoon with a gimpy leg, wrinkled his nose at the odor of human bone. Culdesac got the sense that these feral animals did not fully accept that the town was theirs. Despite the fact that there were plenty of homes to go around, many slept on the roof or the front lawn. Most of the former pets proclaimed ownership over their masters' houses—especially those who could produce a human corpse for the mass grave at the old football field. Many other pets fled, unable to accept a world in which their every need was not met. The farm animals from the nearby ranches ambled along the highway, completely bewildered. A few do-gooders—the dogs, mostly—escorted the refugees into Milton, assuring them that the humans were gone, and that no one would hurt them ever again.

At the perimeter of the safe zone, two torches stood at opposite ends of an intersection, the corner of Main and Booth. Culdesac suspected that Booth was some wealthy landowner who got lucky a century earlier, sunk some money into the town. In the middle of the wide intersection, a statue of a soldier stood on a pedestal, glazed with pigeon dung. The monument commemorated humans who fought in a civil war many decades before. A fountain the size of a child's tub was seated at the base of the pedestal, its vertical pipe no longer spraying water. Dead leaves floated on the surface, while coins glittered on the bottom.

Behind the statue, the charred remains of the post office waited for a strong breeze to knock them over. The fire station across the street lay dormant as well, its only truck stripped for parts by the fleeing humans. Rows of brick storefronts lined the avenue, including a hardware store, a coffee shop, and a pub called Murphy's with a shamrock on its sign. The road lifted

upward at the end of the block, with a church steeple forming
its peak. When the sun rose, the tower would gleam gold and
white, though the bell would remain silent forever.

In the square, Anansi and Seljuk leaned on a stack of crates,
rifles in hand, smoking hand-rolled clove cigarettes. When the
two tomcats smelled Culdesac approaching, they stood at attention. Anansi had jet-black fur, with bright green eyes that seemed
to float in the darkness. Seljuk was a tabby with a white chin,
a little triangle under his mouth that made him resemble an
old human professor. Both wore black armbands imprinted
with the image of a sphinx, a lion with wings and a human
head. The mythical creature that served as the inspiration for
the unit. A guardian of great wisdom who would nevertheless devour those who proved unworthy.

Rather than let them stand at ease, Culdesac decided to
grill them. "What are these crates still doing here?" he asked.
The boxes contained equipment salvaged from previous expe-
ditions, including a roll of copper wire, a ray gun that could
supposedly disable a drone, and a high-powered telescope. All
of it should have been stored in the police station by now.

"We're waiting for orders," Anansi said.

Waiting for orders? "I smell blood," Culdesac said. "You
were supposed to clean out the fire department."

"We did, sir."

"Well?"

Nervously, both cats pointed toward the three-story apart-
ment building. At the base of the building, in the driveway, a
dark patch of blood and gore had splattered all over the concrete and the wall, like some abstract art installation.

"There was a human we missed," Anansi said. "Hiding out in
that building. We got him."

Culdesac nodded. "Get me my Number One."

Seljuk let out a long grunt that ended in a very catlike *yeow*. A code word from their feral days. Seconds later, Mort(e) emerged from the police station, where most of the Red Sphinx slept on the floor, their breath steaming the windows. The cat checked his sidearm as he jogged toward the square. When he was close enough, Mort(e) saluted, revealing once again those hideous, knobby fingers, sheared off at the knuckle by his masters to prevent him from clawing at their precious furniture. To add insult to injury, this former housecat was a choker as well, his balls cut off before he even knew what they were for. This cat, Culdesac's second in command, was a living testament to the depravity of the human age. The Red Sphinx needed him to overcome these disadvantages, to grow strong from them, to channel his hatred from them. If this cat couldn't do that—and Culdesac was still not entirely sure—he would get them all killed sooner or later.

"Report," Culdesac said.

"All is quiet," Mort(e) said. "Citizens are accounted for. A few are out foraging—you may have seen them on your way in."

"What about this mess over here?" Culdesac said, pointing to the blood.

"Sniper opened fire. We took care of him."

"You told me that this town was secure. You told me you searched the houses."

"I know. I'm sorry. He hid his scent from us."

"How?"

Mort(e) exchanged glances with the two guards. When Seljuk started to chuckle, Anansi nudged him.

"He coated his body in Vaseline."

"What?"

"Petroleum jelly. He came out shooting buck-naked. I think he hid in a crawlspace for as long as he could stand it."

"A crawlspace you said you checked?"

"Sir," Anansi said. Culdesac made a big show of opening his eyes in wonder at this foot soldier who spoke out of turn. The last time someone did that, Culdesac asked if he could see the cat's rifle. When the soldier handed it over to him, Culdesac slammed the butt into the cat's stomach, then set the rifle down and walked away.

"Forgive me, sir," Anansi said. "Mort(e) is leaving out the part where he saved our lives."

"Is he now?"

Anansi explained that while the human fired into the town, shouting nonsense the whole time, Mort(e) quietly climbed the side of the building. He snuck onto the roof, grabbed the man from behind, and tossed him over the edge. Oddly, the man continued speaking even in the two seconds of freefall, the concrete shutting his mouth for good.

The Queen herself asked Culdesac to watch over this young recruit, out of all the strays he drafted for the Red Sphinx. Yet again, Mort(e) showed him why. And Culdesac had to wonder: was it his role to keep this cat from going too far? From getting too cocky? At least Mort(e) put his own life before others. But still—how dangerous is the person with nothing to lose? How long could that power be harnessed before it ripped itself free?

"Where's the body?" Culdesac asked. "Why aren't we cooking him for breakfast before the meat goes bad?"

Behind Mort(e), the two soldiers finally let out a breath.

"Tiberius took the body," Mort(e) said. "He wants to know if he can find any traces of EMSAH in the brain."

Culdesac snorted. *Sure, for all the good it'll do*, he thought.

"Those were your orders, correct?" Mort(e) asked. "You wanted us to collect human specimens for examination."

Culdesac smiled, slipped his hand into his pack, and pulled

out the human skull. Under the torches, the bone resembled a polished rock.

"There are exceptions," Culdesac said.

"Is that...*him*?" Mort(e) said.

"Yes. He was delicious. And now I want more."

He told Mort(e) to take him to Tiberius. Later that day, Culdesac would have to speak to the envoy—an exhausting exercise for which he would need another bellyful of hork, or mank, or shank, or whatever it was called.

TIBERIUS COMMANDEERED A sterile, windowless room in the local clinic to use as a morgue. Culdesac entered just as the medic was wrapping up. The fluorescent panels, powered by a portable generator, cast a harsh light on the blue tiled walls and white linoleum floor. The body lay on a metal table, sliced open from the chin to the genitals like a slaughtered animal. Organs glistened in steel pans. A bruise, covered in pink abrasions, spread along the ribs, hip, and thighs, indicating the point of impact. The clavicle and femur protruded from the broken skin. A more deliberate motion had sheared off the top of the cadaver's head, exposing the pink brain. The scalp sat by itself on a counter like a breakfast bowl overflowing with blood.

Tiberius tore the blue rubber gloves from his misshapen hands. He untied his apron, covered in blood, and then removed his facemask. Last to go were his little boot coverings, flecked with red droplets. Underneath, the white fur of his feet tempted Culdesac to address him as Socks, the slave name that the cat despised. But this medic spent a long night alone with this putrid human, whose body odor was almost as pungent as his entrails, overpowering the antiseptic scent of the clinic.

"Good morning, Captain," Tiberius said, saluting with his white paw. "Nice of you to join me and my guest for breakfast."

The lights dimmed, then brightened. Someone must have added more fuel to the generator outside.

"What are you looking for?" Culdesac asked.

"Just performing an autopsy. Trying to determine the cause of death."

"What was it?"

Tiberius glared at him. "I'm joking, sir. He clearly died from the fall."

Socks liked to kid around, even when those around him were in no mood for it.

"Those dogs we found last month," Tiberius said. "They had lesions in their brains. I wanted to see if this human had the same thing. He doesn't. Another waste of time."

The cat folded his arms and leaned against the counter. For months, Tiberius tried to track the causes of the EMSAH Syndrome. When they came across a pack of infected dogs, their bodies huddled under a tree, he begged Culdesac for the chance to examine them. Culdesac gave him free reign. The soldiers found the task of collecting and tagging the bodies a morbid chore, even after months of fighting. They chafed at taking orders from Tiberius, the medic who had once been a pet. But Tiberius performed his task well, and his logbooks and reports became invaluable in the war effort. Officers in the regular army, who typically resented the perks that the Red Sphinx enjoyed, nevertheless requested to meet with Tiberius, to hear his stories from the front. EMSAH was everyone's concern, and the medic was often the first person to encounter and study the disease in the field. Culdesac considered telling him to give it a rest—after all, the Colony was handling all of this, and Tiberius tended to make those around him anxious. But the neverending search kept Tiberius busy and focused. Fighting him on this issue wasn't worth the trouble.

"It's not a waste of time," Culdesac said. "Every person you examine shows us something."

"I hope we're still around to figure out what that *something* is."

Culdesac thought for a moment how the cat would react if he told him the truth: there was no cure for EMSAH. There never would be. It was hopeless. Even the Queen knew this, deep in her heart. Perhaps Culdesac would derive some kind of twisted pleasure from revealing this truth to Tiberius. For now, he would keep it to himself, for the good of everyone.

"Are you still speaking to the envoy today?" Tiberius asked.

"Yes."

"Do you think they'll have us stay here?"

All the soldiers in the Red Sphinx were exhausted. Mort(e) had already cautioned Culdesac about pushing them too hard. And now Tiberius joined the chorus, begging for a few days leave, with the humans on the run and the area secure.

"It depends on the humans," Culdesac said. "They tried to take this town for a reason. And now they're regrouping on the other side of the mountains."

"Wouldn't they be better off going south?" Tiberius was referring to the bay, where a human warship could cover the enemy supply line by taking potshots from over a mile out to sea. If the humans lost that, then these tiny towns would not matter. Their forces would wither and die in this terrain.

"They would be better off surrendering," Culdesac said. "Or driving away in their boats and sitting in the middle of the Atlantic until they starve to death."

"Maybe they're trying to spread EMSAH around as much as they can before they retreat," Tiberius said.

"That makes sense."

No matter what the humans did, they would leave a trail of

misery and death in their wake. Just like before the war. As far as Culdesac could tell, little had changed.

"Well, here's one less human you'll have to worry about," Tiberius said. "Who's on chow duty this week?"

"Logan."

"Oh, he'll screw it up. Get the Texan to cook him. She can turn a pile of dirt into a banquet if she had to." When Tiberius realized he spoke inappropriately, he cleared his throat. "I mean, *please*. Sir. I'm only looking out for the well-being of the unit."

Culdesac smiled. "Don't worry. We'll cook him up right."

Outside, someone shouted. Soldiers ran along the side of the building. Something was happening.

"I'll find the Texan later," Tiberius said.

Culdesac headed for the double doors that led to an alley. There, the voices and footsteps echoed against the concrete and mortar. Culdesac followed them to Booth Street. To his right, soldiers ran through the town square. Mort(e) stood at the base of the statue, directing the cats to fan out along Main and to take cover behind the parked vehicles. Everyone focused on the church, where a stained glass window reflected the glare of the rising sun. Civilians stuck their heads out of windows and stood on rooftops, hoping to catch a glimpse of the action. Culdesac noticed three cats on the ledge of an office building, their pointy ears silhouetted against the brightening clouds.

In the town square, Mort(e) sent Striker and Hennessey on a flanking maneuver. Dread and Rookie would stake out a position in the rear of the church.

"What's happening?" Culdesac asked.

"Someone broke into the church," Mort(e) said. "Not a human. But we told the civilians to stay in the perimeter."

Culdesac checked his sidearm. "Let's go."

His gun drawn, Culdesac led nine soldiers up the street. Ice water pumped through his veins, angering him, quickening his movements. At the top of the hill, more of his cats waited, their rifles propped on the hoods of abandoned cars. In front of the church, a black sign with white letters spelled out the name ST. MICHAEL'S EPISCOPAL, with service times listed underneath. The building was crafted from stone, with a foundational slab listing the date 1852. A set of steps rose to meet a pair of doors, painted crimson with a giant brass knob. Above, at the base of the steeple, an octagonal piece of stained glass depicted a dove flying through a ring of laurels.

"How many entrances?" Culdesac asked.

"Three."

Mort(e) looked at Gai Den, a gray cat wielding a rifle with a bayonet duct-taped to the barrel. When Mort(e) twirled his fingers, Gai Den nodded and raised his hand—a signal to Dread and Striker to enter the building at the side and rear doors.

Culdesac gripped the brass knob and pulled the door open. Mort(e) filled the void, sweeping his pistol from left to right to clear the lobby. Culdesac followed, taking in the musty odor of the carpet. Light streamed in through the stained glass windows, casting rainbow-colored rectangles onto the hickory pews. At the other end of the room sat an altar with a white cloth hanging halfway off of it. Above, the chandeliers dangled from chains connected to wooden rafters. One of them wobbled a bit, revealing how a mere influx of guests could shake the foundation of this old building.

Culdesac slid behind the first row of pews, still aiming ahead. Mort(e) stood next to him. At the front of the room, Striker and Hennessey entered through the side door, taking cover behind the stone pulpit. In the corner behind the altar, another door was built into the wall, with only the knob and the thin seams visible.

On the other side, someone shouted.

Gun raised, Culdesac sprinted up the aisle. Mort(e) and the others padded closely behind. By the time he reached the altar, Striker turned the knob and swung the door open. When Culdesac stepped inside, a powerful stench slapped him the face, making him blink. The room was some kind of storage area, with a desk in the corner that the minister used to stash his vestments, candles, oils, and other sacred objects. Nearby, stacks of wooden crates reached to the ceiling. Dread aimed his rifle in between two of the columns. This cat was one of Culdesac's favorites. Months earlier, a sharp chunk of shrapnel cut into Dread's shoulder, leaving a rough scar that could no longer grow fur. To conceal the injury, he got a tattoo of an ant's head, the antennae sticking out, the jaws open. Culdesac got the sense that Dread wanted another wound so he could add more body art.

"I see you," Dread said. "Come on out."

A pair of furry ears poked over one of the crates.

"These crates are mine," a voice said. Definitely a female, though Culdesac could barely smell with the horrible stench covering over everything.

"This town is under the occupation of the Red Sphinx," Culdesac said. "The crates belong to us."

"Are you going to kill me for them?" the female asked.

"Probably. But if you surrender, we can at least talk about it before we shoot you."

A pause. Culdesac's joke did not go over well.

"Okay, we won't shoot you," he said. "But we're going to secure the area one way or the other."

The cat shuffled out from her hiding spot. She rose on her hind legs to a height taller than the others, almost as tall as Culdesac. Her irises had a golden tinge. Brown, gray, and black stripes cut across her thick coat. Shaggy hair hung from her cheekbones, and a tuft of fur formed a little patch under her chin. Her bushy tail slid out from behind the crate like a python. Culdesac recognized the breed: a Maine coon cat, no doubt raised by wealthy humans to appear feral while at the same time being affectionate, loyal, docile. Like a goddamn dog, almost.

"I know this one, sir," Dread said. "She runs the hotel."

"The Royal Inn," she corrected.

"It's not really a hotel, sir," Dread added, slightly embarrassed.

Culdesac knew the place. A stone's throw away. Some of the soldiers drank there while Culdesac tracked the human in the woods. They even solicited some company for the evening, a transaction no doubt arranged by this cat. Perhaps she had been the owner's pet, reclining on the concierge desk while people waited to check in. She was one of many animals who carved out a comfortable life from the war.

"Who's with you?" Culdesac asked.

"No one," she said.

"What are you doing here?"

"I told you. These crates are mine."

She wore a yellow band on her wrist, indicating that she tested negative for EMSAH. With all the itchy trigger fingers in the room, the band probably saved her life.

Culdesac motioned for someone to open one of the boxes. Striker used his field knife to pry open the top. The smell grew thicker. The Maine coon cat reached her hand inside.

"Back away from it!" Culdesac said. Startled, the cat stepped away.

A layer of dry straw lined the interior of the crates. Striker's hand disappeared up to his forearm as he sifted through it. He pulled a burlap sack from the box, sniffed it, and then grimaced, trying to hold in a sneeze. Culdesac walked over and took it. Spinning the bag around, he saw a logo for Darby Coffee, Ltd. The name appeared stenciled into a circular map of the world.

"Check the others," he said. "Dread, keep an eye on her."

The Maine coon didn't like it, but since she was still alive, she should be grateful.

"Nothing, sir," Striker said.

"Nothing over here," Hennessey said.

Culdesac dropped the bag into its crate. The Maine coon cat watched him.

"I'm Nox," she said.

"What did you expect to do with all of this?"

"Sell it."

"To whom? Only the humans drink this dirt."

"I beg to differ. Our people love this stuff."

Nox explained that the humans attacked soon after the animals in Milton changed. They packed supplies in the church, the most solid structure in the neighborhood. A three-day siege forced the survivors to make a run for it, and leave their rations behind. As one of the leaders of the siege, Nox claimed the spoils. The animals in town had no interest in the smelly brown beans—until she brewed them on her own. And then they couldn't get enough.

"Did the humans attack this town so they could get the coffee?" Culdesac asked.

"It's not as crazy as it sounds," she said. "Some of them are so addicted to it they can't even wake up without it. I'll bet they wanted to take it to their boat. If that ship in the bay has run out coffee, the humans on board are done for."

It made for a funny image in his mind: drowsy humans accidentally steering their mighty warship into a lighthouse.

"So, you were going to turn your brothel into a café?" he asked. The other cats laughed.

"It'll be both," she said. "When the war's over."

When the war's over. So many of these civilians thought that the war was already over simply because their masters were gone, and their worlds expanded beyond their houses or their yards or their farmlands. But there were years of bloodshed to come. No one would be the same when it was over.

"Take her to the perimeter," Culdesac said. "Don't let anyone else out."

Everyone in the room relaxed. Culdesac holstered his gun. Mort(e) took it from there, ordering the cats to file out and return to their base of operations. Dread gripped Nox's arm to pull her along. The Maine coon snapped her elbow out of his hands.

"I have to stay here," she said.

"We're not taking your coffee," Culdesac said.

"*They* will," she said. "The humans. They're coming back, aren't they?"

Culdesac felt several pairs of eyes turn to him.

"I hope so," he said, grinning.

Nox did not smile back.

As the tension eased, the cats filed out through the rear exit. The smell of the coffee followed them outside, billowing through the doorway and pooling in the small courtyard. Surrounded by soldiers, Nox looked at him, her tail standing straight up like a squirrel's.

"Come talk to my soldiers if you need to go outside the perimeter," Culdesac said.

"Thank you."

"Culdesac," he said.

"Culdesac."

"*Captain* Culdesac," Mort(e) chimed in.

"I'll bring you some coffee, Captain," she said.

He had allowed this minor flirtation to drag on long enough. "Don't bother. Just stay in the perimeter so you don't get shot."

Dread snorted, as if to say, *Real smooth, Cap*.

Nox bowed her head, then followed Dread and Hennessey as they escorted her to the town square. Her tail swished with each step. While Mort(e) said something about keeping the civilians inside the perimeter, Culdesac waited for her to look back at him. But she never did.

CHAPTER THREE
THE ENVOY

HE ENVOY ARRIVED later that afternoon, right on schedule. A steady rain moved in, pattering on the grass, dirt, and asphalt like thousands of kittens' paws. Culdesac met the Alpha outside the perimeter, on a small concrete bridge wide enough for a single car to pass. He went alone. The ants seemed to prefer it that way. Culdesac certainly did. The translator that he used to communicate with the ants often left him disoriented. It would take him years to master it. Until then, he did not need his subordinates to see him like that.

The Alpha lumbered down the street, straddling the faded yellow highway stripes. Crawling on all six legs, she was about the size of an average human automobile—if it included a massive head with a jaw like a garbage compactor on the front. The antennae alternated, one flipping up while the other dropped down. Smaller ants swarmed about her skin, forming a symbiotic relationship that kept the Alpha connected to the Colony. For all her weight, her claws padded the concrete without a sound, even stealthier than a cat.

Culdesac readied the translator. The ants made the device out of some unnamable biomaterial that only they could master. In his hands, it resembled the headgear that a radio operator would wear. He fit the earpiece into place, and positioned the speaker in front of his mouth. He extended the antenna as far as it could go.

The Alpha rose up on her hind legs, like a walking tree. She paused there, every limb and joint remaining perfectly still. Her smaller sisters continued flowing over her body, undeterred by the cold rain. Soon, all the ants traveled clockwise around the Alpha's skin, like a contained cyclone.

They were ready to speak to Culdesac.

The Alpha lowered her head. Her antenna dangled over the translator, the two appendages shaking as they reached for each other. To stay focused—to stay sane, really—Culdesac thought of the hunt. Oh, Culdesac missed the hunt. He tried to conjure the forest floor moving underneath his body, the warm smells of mud, urine, and fur. The sounds of chirping and buzzing and wind rustling the leaves.

Before his mind wandered too deep, back to the dark day when he found his brother's mangled corpse, Culdesac lifted his head. The antennae touched, sending a spark into the earpiece that made him open his mouth in a silent scream of madness and ecstasy.

CULDESAC OPENED HIS eyes to a wall of gray fur. An old memory. He was getting better at recognizing that, at distinguishing the real world from the jumbled images of the translator.

He remembered the cat in front of him—a female whose mate strayed into the territory that Culdesac and his brother had claimed. Earlier that day, Murmur and Culdesac cornered the male near the entrance to a cave. The intruder's ragged coat and bony limbs gave him away as one of the desperate ones, someone driven from the hills in search of new hunting grounds. He needed to die. Murmur did most of the work, breaking the cat's scrawny neck with his jaws. When the female came looking for

him, Murmur claimed her. She pawed him away at first. But she
must have smelled her lover on him, and realized that things
had changed. So Murmur took her. Culdesac watched from the
bushes. He growled at Murmur, the way his mother did. Murmur
grunted at him, telling him to keep quiet, his body contorting
over the prone female. When he was finished, Murmur left the
bobcat and continued to pick at the bones of her mate. When
the female spotted Culdesac in the shrubs, she stared at him
with dead eyes, like two raindrops on a leaf. She waited there
as he found the courage to creep toward her, to mount her, to
dig his claws into her protruding ribs while he did it. Though
burned in his memory, the moment lasted mere seconds. He
collapsed onto her after finishing, and sunk his teeth into her
ear. When he bit too hard, she spun around, dislodging him
from inside her. She slashed him hard on his flank, leaving three
hot lines, each oozing blood. He lay on his belly, exhausted and
content even with his wounds. The female wandered off. The
last thing he saw was her tail slinking along a boulder before
disappearing.

An unnatural darkness passed over the forest, like a shade
drawn over a window. Though still out of breath and covered
in the bobcat's scent, Culdesac remembered where he was. He
recalled *who* he was, a warrior in the Queen's army, using a
device that few other animals could master. This memory replay-
ing in his mind was merely the first level. The Queen pulled him
deeper, past this membrane and into her inner chamber, where
everything that anyone had ever known would be revealed.

THE AIR THICKENED around him. Opening his eyes changed nothing—the room in which he found himself was completely cut
off from the light, a hermetically sealed chamber. The spongy
floor below him smelled like the female bobcat, flavoring his

saliva every time he swallowed. All around him, other creatures moved about the room. He recognized them by scent: the
Queen's chambermaids, shuffling about, their antennae probing
him. And soon, he could sense their chemical signals, as if he
were an ant himself. The chemicals entered his bloodstream and
sped through his body, lighting up his nervous system before
taking root in his brain. No emotions. No lies. Only pure truth,
distilled into a handful of molecules that could convey more
information than all the human languages combined. The signals
eliminated the need to see. Here, darkness and light became irrel-
evant, replaced by the pinging echoes of the Queen's revelation.

When the Queen first spoke to him through the translator,
she did so using images and metaphors, memories from his days
before the war. Afterward, he would spend hours piecing them
all together. Now, after months of practice, he could speak to
her directly. He became one of them, a child of the Colony,
freed of his mammalian shackles.

WELCOME, the Queen's voice said. And then she uttered the
name that his mother gave to him, a humming noise at the base
of her throat that only he would recognize. A sound long forgotten until the Queen plucked it from his subconscious. Thus no
secrets remained between them. The Queen became him, and
he became the Queen, a connection that went far beyond the
paltry human concept of love.

I kneel before you as your servant, Culdesac said.

The Queen leaned over him, her antennae brushing his fur.
Her pulsating abdomen dropped eggs that the chambermaids
collected. Here, her aging body, with its cracked skin and calcified joints, gave birth to the future. Life stubbornly persisted,
even in the rotting shell that housed her dark heart and her infinite mind.

YOU WILL RETREAT, the Queen said.

She sensed his confusion. The Red Sphinx had not surrendered conquered territory since the war began. To drive the point home, the Queen revealed an image of the town in flames, the fire rising around the statue of the human soldier, reflected on the filmy surface of the fountain. He watched it through a long tunnel with no sound.

We can fight, he said, though he did not need to. She knew his thoughts.

Once more, the Queen answered with images. He saw the terrain from above, through the eyes of the Queen's many bird patrols. Brown farmlands sectioned off the land to the south, while the forest crept over the broken highway and the fraying edges of the town. Far off, in the rocky highlands, a human army gathered. And then, in a flash, Culdesac could think like the Queen, seeing multiple possibilities unfold at once. The Queen could not predict the future, but she could calculate probabilities better than any computer. Culdesac shuddered as he saw the scenarios layered on top of one another—victories, defeats, stalemates—until everything blurred. She could ram the information into his mammalian brain, but it would take time to understand it.

WITHDRAW, she said. YOU HAVE TWO DAYS.

He needed to say something to her, but did not know how. He concentrated until he conjured up the image of the man he hunted, clutching a flask of whiskey before dying. He heard the hollow flask clank on the ground.

They want the town, he said. Though retreating might serve some greater purpose in the war, it would surrender something the humans considered valuable.

The chambermaids stood still while the Queen pondered this. Even the smells went away, leaving an empty space in Culdesac's mind.

FIND OUT WHY, she said.

Yes.

The Queen sent her daughters out into the world to gather information, to fill in the gaps in her knowledge. All that was unseen was eventually revealed, if given enough time, enough insects crawling into the hidden spaces. For so long, Culdesac served as her sword slashing at the enemy. Now, he would be an instrument of her omniscience, one of her claws reaching into the darkness.

The warmth of the Queen's lair began to fade. A panic set in as Culdesac realized that he was about to be expelled from paradise, from the presence of the Queen who saved him. Some day, she would let him stay. She would reward him for all this suffering and pull him in so deep that he could never leave. He would dissolve into the Colony, his life becoming one with his millions of sisters. He would be a star spiraling around the center of the Queen's galaxy, where he truly belonged.

CULDESAC LOOKED AT his paws as they squished the melting snow. The winter lingered in the hills, decimating the remaining survivors of the latest human incursion. He recognized this time and place, a memory from several months after his first encounter with the female bobcat. He was lean, delirious from hunger. He spent part of the day clawing at a beetle as it burrowed into the earth. And then, desperate for food, he licked the slimy mud from his paws. It filled his gut for few moments before he retched, leaving a hollow feeling in his shriveled stomach.

Someone called his name, from somewhere over the nearest hill. For a moment, Culdesac thought it was the Queen. When he heard it a second time, he recognized his brother's voice. He ran toward the sound, his soaked paws growing chilly. There, a red splash of blood painted the white snow. Murmur dug his face into the carcass of some animal, the ribs exposed. Beside him, two smaller creatures lay dead, their spines crushed. Murmur looked up, acknowledged his brother, and continued eating.

Culdesac recognized the smell. He examined the creature's face, sniffing around it, licking the wound in her neck where Murmur slashed her. It was the female bobcat. Her two kittens lay nearby, their eyes still sealed shut. She strayed into this territory hoping to find a place to bear her young, unaware that Murmur was hunting her. Culdesac stared into the cat's glassy eye and remembered mating with her. An ache formed in his groin, while saliva pooled in his mouth.

Murmur scratched him on his shoulder, enough to draw a trickle of blood. Culdesac's brother wanted this carcass all to himself. If Murmur remembered this bobcat, he did not seem to care.

Culdesac hissed at him, though he would do nothing. Instead, he approached the two kittens. He nudged them with his nose and mumbled at them, but they were beginning to freeze stiff. For all Culdesac knew, these two young ones were his nephews, or his own sons. Something terrible forced their mother to gamble their young lives. Some awful cruelty that Culdesac was only now discovering, both in the world around him, and within himself. With so much taken away from him, he would have to become cruel in response. Hard and unforgiving, like the frozen soil in winter.

But for now, he was starving. And so he did what he needed to do to live another day. And as the cold meat sat in his belly, his thoughts melted away, replaced by the wind and the earth and the trees.

When they finished, only the furry tails and a pile of wet bones remained. Culdesac sniffed the remnants of the female once more, trying to recall the madness of their union. With the sun going down, and the temperature dropping, a heavy snowfall began. They left the carcasses to be buried in the storm. It would hide what they did until the spring.

CULDESAC AWOKE IN a sitting position, leaning on the concrete railing of the bridge. The rain continued to fall. In his dazed state, he stuck out his tongue to catch the drops. The cold water washed away the taste of the bobcat flesh. Culdesac rolled his head to the side in time to catch the Alpha waddling away. She stepped off the road and disappeared into the trees.

Culdesac stood up and propped his elbows on the railing. His senses overwhelmed him. The babbling of the river below throbbed in his eardrums. The brightness of the white clouds seared into his retinas. The roughness of the concrete sent lightning bolts from his fingertips into his gut. His body needed to latch onto the real world in order to shake off the dreams of the translator. It would pass. He would become stronger from it.

CHAPTER FOUR
PSYCHOS

AS TIBERIUS PREDICTED, Texan prepared a lovely feast, a barbecue befitting her name. Logan was demoted to cutting onions and preparing a soup from the bones and gristle. The cats who were off duty ate the meat in the town square. After each bite, the cats licked their paws and rubbed their oily faces, as they did in the days before the Change. With the storm clouds tumbling to the east, they could enjoy the cookout like carefree pets.

Culdesac watched from the corner office of the police station, once occupied by the sheriff. The room remained frozen in time. A calendar on the bulletin board was stuck on a month that had gone terribly for the humans. Next to it, a yellowing flyer warned of ant infestations. A stray bullet left a spider web of cracks in the plaster. Plaques hung on the wall from chest level to the ceiling, honoring the sheriff for his service and bravery. The only new things in the room were the boxes hauled in for storage, each with illegible labels stenciled in white paint.

In the neighboring buildings, the cats standing guard received small pieces of the crazy human. Through the horizontal blinds, Culdesac saw Packer and Hanh sitting on the roof of a school, munching away on their feast, their rifles in their laps. Logan delivered a small helping to Culdesac. The soldiers knew to leave him alone after a session with the translator. He needed the time to ponder not only what the Queen said, but the messages embedded in the images, the smells, the sounds. Typically, his journeys into the Queen's world dropped him into pitched battles, where the ants raided human strongholds or hunted prey in the wild. He felt safer there. He could act rather than talk. He could kill rather than negotiate. This surreal memory of his brother, on the other hand, left him confused. Perhaps the Queen wished to remind him of how vulnerable he could be right before ordering him to retreat. She wanted to show him that some problems yielded no solutions, forcing him to choose between bad and worse.

A few of the townsfolk gathered around the square, most likely attracted to the smell, but also curious about this band of feline warriors. Culdesac counted a family of squirrels, a few dogs and cats, a raccoon, a rabbit. As the only all-feline unit in the army, answering directly to the Queen, the Red Sphinx earned a reputation among the animals. But here, the fearsome soldiers played games with the children. Bailarina kicked a soccer ball along the cobblestone street with two kittens. One of them pointed to her gun, and she told him that it was not a toy. When a kitten slipped and fell on the wet stones, Bailarina helped him to his feet and brushed the dirt from his fur. Nearby, Folsom let a puppy wear his helmet. A few sizes too big, the helmet covered the dog's eyes, making her giggle and wag her tail. Soon the other children wanted to try it on.

Culdesac decided to wait until after the meal to tell his soldiers about the Queen's order to retreat. They needed to enjoy this down time. With the meat rumbling in his stomach, he turned to the map on his desk. As he flattened it out, he found the town of Milton, a densely packed blob of squares connected to the gray string of the turnpike. Culdesac traced his finger along the blue line until he came across a trail that ended at the water. With a brown marker, he drew a straight line through it. Then, switching to red, he wrote "The Lick" above it.

Beyond the river, the forest widened. Somewhere out there, in the same place he once called home, the humans prepared to march on his position. The Queen once told him that they would grow only more dangerous when cornered. Animals at least cared if they lived or died, and they rarely killed for sport. Humans, on the other hand, were easily pushed to extremes, even in the wars they were winning.

Despite the Queen's orders, he could not resist thinking of a way to defend the town. He wanted to get the full view of the terrain from the church steeple, the highest point. With the map tucked under his arm, he exited the back door of the station, which opened onto a side street. Heading toward the church, he could hear the laughter and banter in the square. Kicking around the soccer ball must have turned into a full-fledged game, judging from the shouts and scuffling feet. Someone scored, and a great roar went up, followed by clapping and more laughter.

He entered the church of St. Michael's through the storage area, overwhelmed once again by the smell of the coffee crates. He found the staircase to the steeple—a creaking, wooden spiral with two of the steps missing. Culdesac kicked the bottom step three times, then twice more. The sentry on duty responded with the same series of knocks, letting Culdesac know that he could ascend the staircase without getting shot. At the top, a cat named Dutch saluted him. She had bright white fur, with a pair of binoculars hanging from a strap around her neck. The company sniper rifle rested on the railing. Dutch joined the Red Sphinx in the depths of winter, when her pristine coat made her virtually invisible in the snow. In these warmer months, she needed to improvise, though she never found a human jacket that fit her right.

"Nothing to report, sir," she said.

"Good. Go get something to eat."

"Sir?"

"I'll keep watch."

Culdesac had all of his soldiers trained to think that any act of kindness on his part constituted a miracle. Dutch thanked him, saluted again, and hurried down the steps. She was supposed to confirm that the rifle was ready and loaded, but Culdesac let it go.

He sat beside the bell and wrapped his knuckles on it, expecting a hollow *bong* sound. Instead, the dense metal hardly produced any noise at all. He unfolded the map on his knees and gazed out at the countryside. Extending his arm and sticking his thumb in the air, he pointed out the two peaks that rose about three miles away. The animals renamed them the Weavers, in honor of an ant species. The Pharaohs and the Honeypots stood in the other direction. The human soldiers under General Fitzpatrick camped in the hills, where the dense granite surface prevented the Alphas from bursting through the soil to snatch them up.

Culdesac heard a door slam downstairs. He wondered if it was Dutch, but after checking the town square, he saw her standing around the barbecue pit, her white fur like the skin of a ghost. Someone was coming up the stairs. Culdesac sniffed, but the stench of coffee threw him off. He wondered if it would have a permanent effect on his sense of smell.

Someone placed a foot on the first step. Culdesac waited for the signal. When none came, he grabbed the sniper rifle and eased into a kneeling position, with the barrel aiming into the void.

"Hello?" a voice called.

It was the brothel owner, Nox. When she stepped into

view, her eyes widened at the barrel of the gun. But she did not
retreat, or even flinch. Instead, she lifted both hands. In one of
them she held a plastic thermos; in the other, a pair of Styro-
foam cups. A nylon purse hung from her shoulder, too small to
carry a weapon that could do any damage.

"Put those things on the step in front of you," Culdesac said.

She did as she was told. "It's just coffee."

"Who let you outside of the perimeter?"

"The orange one. With the stubby fingers."

Mort(e). As one of the few neutered cats in the Red Sphinx, he
had little interest in what went on at the Royal Inn. Still, Tiberius
and the others must have egged him on to let this female walk
around as she pleased, distracting everyone. Culdesac's Number
One had a decent sense of humor, for a choker.

"Have you really never tried coffee before?" she asked. "You
look tired. This will perk you up."

"I'm not interested."

"Come on, I told you about the humans drinking this stuff.
Don't you want to know what the fuss is about?"

She at last made some sense. But he could not let her have
her way so easily. "You drink it first," he said.

"That is really rude."

"So is shooting you."

Sitting at the top of the steps, she removed the cap and poured
a serving. The aroma remained strong even with a breeze whistling through the steeple. She blew on the surface of the drink
before taking a sip. Then she poured the other cup and offered
it to Culdesac.

"Take a drink of that one, too," he said. She tasted it with a
smile, to let him know how much she enjoyed taking part of his
share. He knew he was being paranoid, but the idea of dying
from a poisoned cup was simply too odious.

When she poured him another, Culdesac leaned the rifle on the railing and accepted more graciously this time.

"Now, take a sip of it like that," she said. "But then try it with this."

Nox unzipped the purse and pulled out a small plastic bottle filled with milk. She then turned the purse over and dumped out a handful of sugar packets.

"Where did you get the milk?" Culdesac asked. All the perishables rotted months earlier, when most of the power grid went out.

"It's mine," she said.

Culdesac responded with a long stare.

"Now we're going to find out what kind of cat you are," she said.

Culdesac slurped it, letting the liquid dissipate so that it would not burn his tongue. It was ghastly, like water tinged with lead. Somehow it tasted worse than it smelled, as if the vapor became liquefied rust. He smacked his lips a few times to air out his mouth.

Nox shook her head. "All right, Captain, try some of this." She emptied half a packet of the sugar into the coffee. She stirred it with her finger, then sucked the excess. He grimaced.

"What, are you a germophobe now?" she asked. The next mouthful tasted even worse. The sugar merely dulled the bitterness, turning the coffee bland.

"Okay, last chance," she said, pouring a few drops of milk into his cup. The creamy whiteness swirled like a cloud at night. These two liquids did not belong together. Sure enough, his next swallow confirmed it. The milk coated his tongue and gums, infused with the coffee. He fought the urge to spit it all out.

"I knew it," Nox said. "Black is your favorite."

"I wouldn't say 'favorite.'"

"Oh, it will be. Once you drink enough of it."

"I suppose I could acquire the taste of my own piss if I drank enough of it."

"Oh, stop. Come on, don't you feel the dark roast working its magic? The humans who lived on this continent thousands of years ago used coffee to stay alert when they were hunting."

Culdesac knew this. Thanks to the translator, he knew almost everything, though he tried to pretend he didn't so as not to scare the civilians. Regardless, Nox made a good point. He did feel more awake. The hot beverage opened his sinuses, at least. He placed the cup on the ledge, and she refilled it.

"Was this illegal once?" he asked. "Like alcohol?"

"No. But I suspect Milton would have been involved in the black market if it had."

"You said this would predict what kind of person I am."

"Sugar means you're friendly, that you love being around people," Nox said. "Milk is more for introverts. But it also means you're a nurturer. You put other people ahead of yourself."

"And black?'

"Black is for psychopaths."

Culdesac folded his arms.

"Really," she said, giggling. "The humans did studies on it."

"Fine," he said. "What's *your* preference?"

"Black."

THEY SAT TOGETHER, like two old friends, and talked about their lives before the war. With the laughter rising from the town square, and the smell of food carried in the breeze, this reprieve almost felt natural. As if this was how things were supposed to be. The Queen could have told him about this cat in the last translator session, but she let him discover Nox on his own. For once,

Culdesac did not see the immediate future, and waded through the present like anyone else.

Still, as was his nature, Culdesac treated it like any other battle. This house pet wanted something from him, and he owed it to the Queen to find out. As Nox spoke, revealing truths about herself both large and small, he waited and watched, probing for weaknesses, preparing to strike or flee if the situation called for it. The art of war in a mere conversation. He took note of the time that passed, stealing glances at his soldiers on the street below. He took note of his own condition. The caffeine seemed to be working, giving him a surreal alertness similar to the lucid dream of the translator.

But Nox came prepared as well. When he asked her about any potential weapons depots in the town, her whiskers twitched. "If you're trying to get some kind of tactical information out of me, you can forget it," she said. "I never even saw a gun until a few months ago."

She admitted that she kept her slave name. She didn't see much point in changing it—not with so many in the town knowing who she was.

"And who *were* you?" Culdesac asked.

There was a nursing home a few blocks from the church. Some rich family donated the property to the town, which included a mansion, a garden, and a small wooded area that the humans believed was haunted with the ghosts of slaves who escaped from the south. The nursing home housed some of Milton's most prominent senior citizens alongside the destitute. Here, all the humans were finally equal as they waited for death to pay a visit. As a result, the home experienced all sorts of problems, from a high turnover rate among the staff to fistfights among the residents. There even existed a kind of wheelchair gang, a cabal of elders who ran the place under the noses of the administrators, dictating who could watch television in the common area, who had phone privileges, even who fucked who. Then a new administrator took over—a young woman named Chandra who was raised in Milton, studied at some big university, and then returned to her hometown. People resented her at first, but she took on a job that no one wanted, at a salary no one else would accept.

Chandra proposed a brilliant idea that solved almost all of the home's problems overnight. The home would serve as both a daycare center and animal shelter. That way, the old people would have something useful to do, rather than bickering over noise levels and bathroom time. Some residents even brought their pets with them when they moved in. Twice a day, the animals were let loose so that both the children and the old people could play with them. The pets jumped about, licking faces, snuggling, sitting in people's laps. After all that, both the children and the residents were so worn out that they all needed naps.

Nox was one of the favorites, thanks to her bushy tail and thick, fluffy coat. A close second was Maynard, the Chihuahua with paralyzed hind legs. His owner—a man named Paulie who became a resident at the home—constructed a harness with two wheels, allowing Maynard to roll around using his front paws while his dead legs dangled behind him. Nox referred to the dog as her brother, and simply ignored Culdesac when he squinted suspiciously at her.

One day, the humans all disappeared, leaving the animals in their cages. Nox was among the first to change. Her newfound strength allowed her to kick the steel gate open and crawl out. The others transformed over the next twenty-four hours. Maynard ditched his harness for a wheelchair, and quickly developed a reputation for his foul language and pushy behavior. His antics grew tiresome, but he was among the smartest as well, having been exposed to the humans the most.

Culdesac caught himself grinning as Nox described that first day of freedom, walking around the town, seeing it for the first time. Even the mundane stories from the house pets filled him with awe at the Queen's power.

By the time Nox finished, the taste of the lukewarm coffee went bland—perhaps because the first few sips burned the top layer of his tongue. With the flavor rapidly dispersing, he found himself craving that first kick. He held out his cup for more.

"I was a breeder," Nox said, topping him off. "My owners rented me out." It made sense for her to get into the same business, more or less. Other towns had trouble dealing with the army regulars when they passed through on their way to the front. But the brothel at the Royal Inn gave the soldiers an outlet. Before the war, Nox was nobody. Lower than a house slave—a womb to be discarded the moment it failed to produce offspring. Now, the people depended on her. Especially the females whom she watched over, and who had nowhere else to go. Nox employed whores of every species. She called them her ladies. Some of them came from the nursing home cages, while the rest filtered in from the streets, and from the wilderness beyond.

"If the humans come for the Royal Inn," she said, "they'll have to kill me for it."

Nox may have wanted something from Culdesac. She may have been trying to manipulate him somehow. But he admired her defiance, the bitterness that chilled her voice. She pulled herself from the darkness, like he had. She deserved to know the truth.

"We've been ordered to evacuate the town," he said.

"Evacuate? Why? I thought we were winning."

He tried to explain that holding a town like this offered little reward, and grave risks. There were too many weak points in a town designed for human comforts and little else.

"We sealed up the sewers," Nox said proudly. "We chased the humans away. We know what we're doing."

"There's a larger strategy to consider here," Culdesasc said. "The Queen sees things that we can't."

"She can predict the future?"

"No. That's impossible. But she's been right every time so far."

"What happens if I say no?"

"You can say no all you want. We'll drag you. Or gag you. Or shoot you, if you leave us no choice."

"My ladies and I are not leaving."

"Do you want your ladies to die?"

"You don't understand."

She promised the people of Milton that the town was theirs. The new leaders even formed a council, consisting of Nox, Maynard, a Labrador named Jack, and the matriarch of a rat clan named Isabel. They planned to engrave a declaration of sovereignty at the base of the war memorial.

"That will have to wait," Culdesac said.

"Wait? You know what the humans are doing. They're burning their cities as they retreat."

"The Queen may have a surprise for them," he said. "And besides: Is it worth your life?"

"As a matter of fact, it is."

"I'm sorry," he said. He meant it.

Culdesac stood up. He chugged the rest of the coffee and flattened his palms on the railing and gazed at the town square. Feeling the prickly sense of being watched, Culdesac lifted the rifle and peered into the scope.

"The town council is not going to roll over," Nox said.

"The town council," he sneered. Culdesac scanned the crowd gathered at the fountain. A wisp of smoke corkscrewed upward from the barbecue pit.

"Are you listening?" Nox asked.

Culdesac centered the crosshairs on a cat with a tuxedo coat, holding a pair of binoculars to his eyes. The lenses glinted in the light. It was Tiberius, the nosy doctor. Upon being spotted, the cat lowered his binoculars. Culdesac thought about squeezing off a round, maybe zipping it over the cat's ears.

This had gone far enough. His own soldiers laughed while Culdesac wasted time with this brothel keeper. The cats must have sent her so they could place bets on whether he would procure her services right there in the steeple.

"Go to the orange cat," he said, setting the rifle on the railing. "The choker with the stubby fingers. Tell him to send the next guard to the tower."

She gaped at this non sequitur. "What about the town?"

"We're leaving. The decision is final."

"Fine, leave. We'll fend for ourselves."

"We can't let the humans capture any prisoners. They know too much as it is."

"We can hide."

"I don't care."

"I heard that this war was about freedom," she said, puffing out her chest. "I heard that we didn't have to take orders anymore. That we could live for ourselves."

"When the war's over," he said, throwing her fantasy in her face. If he had his way, the war would never end, not in his lifetime. Peace would only grind him down, turn him into a rusty hulk of his former self. The war kept him sharp. It made him useful and gave him a purpose. Whatever peace was, it would have to fall to some other generation, a people who never saw their brothers torn to pieces, the scraps piled in a heap.

Squinting, Nox set the thermos on the floor. "Enjoy the rest, Captain." He knew she had more to say, but she did him the courtesy of leaving with no complaint. He took in a deep breath to catch the last hints of her scent. Once again, the oppressive coffee overpowered him. With nothing to do but wait to be relieved, he realized that he needed a *little* more of the coffee. It wasn't so bad. And he already felt more alert than he had in days.

CULDESAC WAITED IN the sheriff's office. He tried to sit. Grew too fidgety, needed to stand. He tapped his foot. Tap-tap-tap. *Where is that choker*, he wondered. His heart shuddered rather than pumped, like an old generator. His breathing quickened. Tried to inhale through his nose. The sound grew too loud. Like waves crashing and never receding. He could not get enough oxygen to match his heart.

The door clicked open. Mort(e) entered.

"What took you so long?" Culdesac said.

"Sorry, sir," the cat said, saluting. "I came as soon as I heard."

"We're leaving," Culdesac said. His tail danced behind him, seemingly of its own accord.

"Leaving?"

"Tomorrow. Queen's orders. Get everyone ready." Culdesac told him to clean out the morgue. To round up the civilians. They would go to the Pharaohs first—the mountains had a cave system. Smash anyone in the face who said no. He slapped his hand on the desk when he said it. The sound made Mort(e) jump. Start at the whorehouse, Culdesac said. Right now—before Nox could tell her employees. No negotiating. No debates. The people will leave with what they could carry. No more.

"Are you all right, sir?" Mort(e) asked.

I'm fine, Culdesac thought. *Of course I'm fine. Nothing's wrong with me. What's wrong with* you*? Can't you take my orders and salute? Just do that. Just say yes.* And then Culdesac realized that he said those words along with thinking them. The connection between his brain and his mouth had short-circuited somehow.

"I'll get started," Mort(e) said.

"Yes, get started." Culdesac tried to say it slowly, to make sure he didn't jump the gun, but the words toppled out end over end.

Mort(e) left. Culdesac could hear him shouting orders outside. His heart wobbled in his chest, sending waves of blood to his limbs, into his stomach, into his brain. That whoremonger must have put something in his drink. Who did she think she was? Just showing up like that. He could have killed her. Right there. A beautiful cat, dead. They wouldn't even clean it up either—just leave it for the town council to find. The town council. What kind of town council has a mistress and a cripple and a rat? What do they even do? *I don't know.* They think they can say no to the Queen? Do they know there's a war going on? We're in a war here. These civilians don't even understand. No wonder. Most of them were pets. They have no idea what it's like. They never needed to forage or hunt. They stood near a bowl and whined. Or they stuck out a paw, or obeyed some cheap command. What did they know?

His mind still spinning, Culdesac imagined a shouting match with Nox in which he asked her, over and over, if she ever saw someone get butchered by humans. Skinned and shredded and left in the mud for the flies and the vermin. *You think you're so smart*, he caught himself saying again and again, each time with an inflection on a different word.

He needed to burn this energy somehow. Like a housecat, he hooked his claws onto the side of the sheriff's desk and scratched it furiously, until he could feel his shoulder blades straining, until he could smell the exposed wood. A pile of shavings gathered at the corner of the desk, and still he kept going. His mind emptied. The noises outside dissolved, drowned out by the incessant scratching.

And then, it stopped. He simply did not need to do it anymore. The room stayed in place. The buzzing in his head died out. He suddenly felt very sleepy, which annoyed him given how much work needed to be done. His next thought annoyed him even more: if only he could have another cup of that horrible coffee, he'd feel awake again.

CHAPTER FIVE
BIRD OF PREY

THE PREPARATIONS CARRIED on into the evening, well ahead of schedule. The Red Sphinx went door-to-door to warn of the looming evacuation. The people of Milton would have to take what they could carry and meet by the statue at first light the next day. Meanwhile, Mort(e) assembled a team to sweep the houses outside the perimeter, to find any squatters who recently latched on to the settlement. So far, they discovered a family of squirrels and two old dogs, brother and sister, who fled from a farmhouse several miles away. From the sheriff's office, Culdesac could hear some of the civilians arguing, demanding that they be given more time. Rumors spread quickly about the humans marching on the town, most likely to burn it. Or infect it with EMSAH, in which case the Colony would have to burn it anyway. Maybe one day, far in the future, they could continue building their settlement. But not yet. It was too soon to celebrate victory over the humans. They would join all the other refugees, herded into safe zones or conscripted into the army.

Tiberius needed two volunteers to help him clean the morgue. It was vital to the war effort that the humans not find out about his experiments. If the enemy discovered that the animals were actively searching for a cure for EMSAH, they could refashion the virus into a new strain, forcing the animals to start all over again. Tiberius initially recruited Riker to help with scrubbing the floors, burning the biohazard materials, and burying the human bones. When Culdesac passed by the facility, he saw Riker vomiting into a row of overgrown bushes. Tiberius finished the rest by himself, leaving the morgue spotless and stinking of bleach.

The situation at the Royal Inn required some diplomacy. Mort(e) interpreted Culdesac's orders as a license to storm the place with three soldiers, waving guns around and telling the patrons that the party was over. When Culdesac heard the commotion all the way in the town square, he rushed to the scene. The saloon section of the Royal Inn had once been an Irish pub, with its front doors and window awnings painted Kelly green, and a faded four-leaf clover on the wall. Located inside the perimeter, only a block from the church, the bar probably served as a nuisance to the human clerics on their holy days. Inside, Mort(e) and his subordinates stood in a row, rifles in hand. With the curtains drawn, oil lamps provided an eerie light in the room. Nox stood behind the bar, holding a double-barreled shotgun. Behind her, a greasy mirror hung from the wall, with a row of ancient liquor bottles lining the counter in front of it.

Patrons of various species stared at the unwelcome guests. Someone had overturned a table. A dog sat on a barstool, his tail to the action, still nursing a glass of bourbon. Next to him, one of the prostitutes stood with her arms draped around the shoulders of an old cat with a gray muzzle. The female wore a fedora—she probably snatched it playfully from the cat's head and wore it while she flirted with him.

Above the bar, several of Nox's ladies rested their elbows on the railing of the balcony to get a view of the show. Each wore oil in her fur to make it shinier, thicker. A female French poodle twisted a gold ring on her middle finger. Two of the cats wore jangling necklaces and bracelets. Of all the smells in the place—wood, booze, cigar smoke—the scent of felines in heat cut through and found its way to Culdesac's nose, taking him back to his days in the wild.

"Are your soldiers going to start shooting if we don't obey?" Nox asked.

She needed to look tough in front of her ladies. Culdesac sympathized, but he did not have time for it. "Put the gun down," he said.

"You think you can just walk in here and—"

"Put! The gun! Down!" Culdesac did not enjoy raising his voice. But he liked seeing the people jump at the sound of it.

Nox slammed the shotgun on the bar, knocking over a few glasses. She folded her arms.

Culdesac turned to Mort(e). "Wait outside." The cats filed out the door. Tension drained from the room. A few people sighed.

"You know the situation," Culdesac announced. "The Colony has issued a direct order to evacuate this town."

"You speak for the Queen?" someone shouted from the balcony.

"I speak *to* the Queen." A few of them knew what he meant. "You can spend your last day here getting ready to leave. Or you can spend it drinking and fucking. That's up to you. Either way, this bar *will* be empty before sunrise."

He supposed that keeping the biggest troublemakers busy at the whorehouse was preferable to trying to detain them. No need for fighting when more peaceful methods produced the same results. If these people obeyed, then he would get his way without firing a shot. If they did not, then he would return in the morning and publicly execute one of them per minute until they complied. No matter the outcome, he would be proven right.

The music started up again, though at a lower volume. On his way out, Nox caught up with him. Mort(e) and his underlings turned, all of them pointing their rifles. Culdesac told them to keep walking. He would follow soon enough. Mort(e), ever the loyal Number One, was the last to obey.

"Thank you," Nox whispered. Her fluffy tail curled over her shoulder.

"Clear out this evening, like I said."

The tip of her tail hid behind her once again.

She waited for him to say something else. When he didn't, she nodded and went inside. The noise leaked from the entrance for a few seconds. The door closed, muffling the music to a low growl, like an animal mumbling in its sleep.

CULDESAC WENT ABOUT gathering his belongings at the sheriff's office. First, he loaded his firearms onto his harness: a sniper rifle, a submachine gun to go along with the pistol he wore on his belt. Then, his toiletries: a swab to pull wax from his ears, a pick to pry debris from his fangs, a vial of salt that he added to water to rinse out his mouth. He cleared the desk of the papers on which he jotted notes and drew doodles, some of which depicted images from the translator sessions. He placed them in a metal trashcan by the window and set them on fire.

When he opened the window to let out the smoke, he noticed a pair of pointy dog's ears poking above the windowsill. They glided across, making it appear that their owner floated rather than walked. Culdesac heard someone arguing in the lobby. This visitor tried to talk his way past Uzi, who guarded the main entrance.

Culdesac walked outside to find Uzi standing stiffly, her rifle held diagonally across her chest. A young alley cat, Uzi's tortoiseshell coat included brown and black patches. Her unique beauty left her no choice but to give herself a scary name. In front of her sat a dog in a wheelchair who must have been Maynard, Nox's brother.

"I'm sorry for the noise, Captain," Uzi said. "This person is about to leave."

"No I'm not!" Maynard said. "I'm from the town council. I'm here to talk to the bobcat." The Chihuahua was smaller than his canine brethren, barely a dog at all, with a large head and a thin snout. He slouched in his chair, resting his paws on the handlebars as if sitting on a throne. A blanket covered his paralyzed legs. He had tan fur and bulging brown eyes, like a grotesque doll. His graying snout and gravelly voice suggested that his days were numbered. So many dog years spent as a slave, and now most likely to die during the evacuation. This civilized world they were building could protect weaker ones like Maynard, but perhaps it kept him alive for too long, prolonging the suffering that a quick kill from a predator would end in an instant.

"I let the Royal Inn stay open," Culdesac said. "What else do you want?"

"Do I look like I care about the fucking whorehouse?" the dog asked. "I'm worse than a choker over here."

Uzi snickered.

"Yeah, that's funny, isn't it?" the dog said. "You're not exactly the brains of this operation, are ya, honey? They let you pretend to be a soldier while they think about shaggin' ya."

Uzi lifted the butt of her rifle, preparing to ram it straight through this loudmouth's face. Culdesac stepped in between them. It had been a while since someone so small mouthed off to him like this. Culdesac almost missed it.

"Do you know who we are?" he asked, smiling with exposed fangs.

"It doesn't matter who you are," Maynard said. "You're about to make a big mistake, leaving this town."

"Is that so? Did you learn military tactics at the nursing home where you grew up?"

"I learned some common sense."

"The decision is final."

"The decision is final," the dog repeated. "We took this town fair and square. It's ours."

Uzi rolled her eyes.

"I've already discussed this with your friend," Culdesac said.

"My *sister*, right. She tried to sweet-talk you."

"She tried."

"I guess those testicles are wasted on a freak like you," the dog said. "Well, if Nox couldn't make it clear, let me try. Abandoning this town will be a disaster."

"You know something the Queen doesn't?"

"Maybe. We've got the bridge, the river, the police station. We've got high points to watch over the entire valley. The humans are going to lose this war. But if they take Milton, it's going to create problems. That's why they want it so bad. Can you get that through your feline skull?"

Under normal circumstances, Culdesac would have killed this dog by now. But Maynard made a few good points. And the Queen herself admitted that she needed more intelligence on this area.

"If you're not going to leave us behind, then stay here and fight with us," Maynard said. "Give us some guns."

"Sure. Maybe we can let you use a bazooka."

"Fuck you, you fucking feral! You fucking choke-dick." The Chihuahua bared his fangs. "You think you're so tough because you grew up in the wild. I'll bet that's not even true. You prob-ably ate scraps from some old lady's garbage."

"That is true," Culdesac said. Uzi turned to him, surprised. "But then I ate the old lady."

"You *know* that we should stay and fight," Maynard said. "I've heard that dumbass motto you use. 'Aim true. Stay on the hunt.' And here you are, hiding behind orders like some human. Remember that a dog in a wheelchair told you that."

Maynard spun the chair and rolled away, the gravel grind-ing under the plastic wheels. When he reached the street, a cat spotted him and offered to help. Maynard waved her off. He stubbornly rolled the wheels, occasionally glancing at the police station and cursing.

Culdesac went inside before Uzi could say anything. He could not wait to leave this town. This was exactly why the Red Sphinx could not occupy a place like this. They were assassins, not administrators and diplomats. Best to leave that thankless work to the regular army. In another week, Culdesac would be on the hunt again, where he belonged.

THAT NIGHT, THE sheriff's office proved far too cold to serve as a bedroom. Culdesac curled into a corner and wrapped himself in blankets. When this failed to work, he decided to sleep with the rest of the unit in the main lobby, where their collective body heat warmed the room. When he arrived, the soldiers grew quiet, surprised that the captain would join them.

Quilted blankets lined the linoleum floor, providing some comfort in this unnatural human space. Culdesac slept back-to-back with Bailarina. His paws rested on Brutal's shoulder, his tail on Rao's neck. Bentley's hind legs twitched in front of Culde-sac's face. This was how his people were meant to end each day. If not for the Queen, he would never have the opportunity to do this ever again. The humans whittled his people down, scattering them, until they lived on their own, groping for warmth in caves or hollow logs. Simple acts such as this reclaimed their past, in defiance of the human juggernaut.

Culdesac dreamt of snow, as he often did. Whiteness in all directions, though without the cold. His brother Murmur growled nearby. Culdesac shouted in response, in the same way his mother did, but Murmur's voice went silent. Only the wind made a sound, shaking wet clumps of snow from the tree branches. Culdesac licked a pile of it until his tongue grew numb.

He awoke in an awkward position, with his head tilted off of his blanket, his tongue dry and stiff, stuck to the floor. Feet padded around his head. Somewhere outside, a clicking sound rattled against the windows, like very loud crickets. The sound came from the sentries tapping two hollow sticks together—a warning that something, or someone, had breached the perimeter.

Culdesac pushed himself up. Within seconds, a groggy Uzi handed him his pistol and a bandolier. Mort(e) greeted him when he stepped outside. Only then did he estimate the time— definitely past midnight, judging by the chill and the position of the half-moon. Candles flickered in the windows of the houses as the civilians woke. Voices and light jazz music drifted from the brothel. Culdesac considered the possibility of rounding everyone up and marching west, now that no one would get any sleep.

"Found a raft anchored in the river," Mort(e) said. "Near the bridge. The guards could smell humans."

Culdesac nodded. He tried to calculate how far the intruders could have gone in two hours, in three, in four.

"Did you search the bridge for explosives?" Culdesac asked.

"Yes. It's clean. But there are no tracks leading from the boat."

"A decoy?"

"Could be. Or they swam downstream from the anchor point."

"Too cold for that."

Jomo sprinted toward them, leaping a row of bushes. "Sir! The brothel has been cleared out."

"Headcount?" Mort(e) asked.

"Ninety of ninety-seven civilians accounted for."

"Get everyone into the station."

The police station could hold these people for a night, maybe into the next afternoon, before they started going crazy. In his initial recon of the town, Culdesac reluctantly concluded that the station would be better than the school, part of which collapsed following a battle in the early days of the Change. To be sure, the station also included jail cells—not exactly a welcoming environment, but safe enough.

Out of the corner of his eye, a white glow rose over the rooftops. At first, it resembled a pair of headlights cresting a hill. Then the light spread, like a sunrise, an unholy magic in the dead of night. The steeple of St. Michael's gleamed so bright it hurt Culdesac's eyes. Pitch-black shadows spilled onto the concrete like an oil slick. None of it made sense—a galaxy's worth of light in such a small space. Desperate for an explanation, Culdesac wondered if his soldiers had pulled some kind of prank. Tiberius probably got his hands on a stash of firecrackers or something. That had to be it.

A mere second passed before the sound of the explosion roared in Culdesac's ears. The shockwave hit him in his chest. He staggered but stayed on his feet. Everyone on the street craned their necks to watch the tower of flame rising into the sky. The white blast dimmed to an orange glow, casting everything before it in silhouette. As the warmth from the fire spread across his face, Culdesac realized that the explosion originated near the edge of the perimeter. At the Royal Inn.

Culdesac was running before he fully understood what was in front of him. The fire crackled, while shards of glass and debris clattered on sidewalks. When he arrived, the staff and patrons of the Royal Inn lay on the ground, moaning. The old cat with the fedora dusted the bits of glass from his fur. One of the feline prostitutes sat on the sidewalk with her arms wrapped around her knees, shivering, while two of her friends tried to comfort her by stroking her head. Several members of the Red Sphinx got to their feet. Culdesac recognized Rao from her gray coat and black armband. She managed to salute him, and to give a nod to show that she was okay.

The Inn had burst open to reveal the depths of hell inside. The wooden beams that supported the structure burned red in the fire, while the charred sign slumped against the splintered front door.

Behind him, Mort(e) asked Rao what happened.

"We got the civilians out," she said. "We were about to do another sweep when the bomb went off."

Mort(e) asked her if they left anyone inside. When she did not answer, Mort(e) grabbed her by the scruff of the neck. "Who was inside?"

"Seljuk," Rao whispered over the crackling of the flames.

A buzzing sound approached from the hills beyond the town. Culdesac knew it well: a drone, circling in from the north, flying low, searching for another target. He once heard that the flying robot's electronic eye could read a license plate from three miles away.

The buzzing dissolved into a low rumbling in his ears when

Culdesac spotted Nox, the only person standing still amidst the movement. She stared at the flames as her beloved Royal Inn burned to the ground. Her home. Her dream, reduced to an ash so fine that it floated away in the breeze. She would breathe it in. It would seep into her blood. When she turned to him, the fire pooling in her eyes, he saw in her all the rage and sadness of his people, the sigh of defeat at the hands of an implacable enemy.

"Captain, the drone," Mort(e) said.

"I hear it."

The humans who operated this machine from afar intended to take out as many animals as possible. This drone had one, maybe two shots left before it would have to return to its landing site.

Nox stared at him, pleading for him to do something.

Culdesac turned and ran to the police station, where the jamming device waited in its padded crate. There, under his orders, the soldiers herded the civilians through the large double doors. But the people stopped to stare at the flames that engulfed the Royal Inn.

"Get away!" he screamed. "Get away from it!"

Only a few of the people actually tilted their heads from the fire to acknowledge him. Culdesac growled. Too many people were like this, content to stand around while their lives bled away. Even after the Change, these pets still needed to learn to fight death, to claw and bite at it, to find life in that ultimately pointless struggle.

Culdesac would save these people anyway. The Queen lifted him from the dirt for that very purpose.

"Incoming!" he said. "Incoming!"

The crowd split apart to give him space. He raced inside, down the corridor to the sheriff's office. He found the crate, flipped the

latches, and opened it. Made of white plastic, the device sat in a
foam casing, resembling a rifle with its barrel, stock, and trigger.
A metal cone was fastened at the end of the barrel, making it
resemble an ancient blunderbuss. He removed the device, along
with a battery pack. When he jammed the pack into a slot, a green
light switched on. The device hummed in his hands.

Culdesac headed for the stairwell. On the way, Uzi stumbled
into his path.

"Sir, we—"

"Get out of the way!" he said, shoving her.

Culdesac followed the stairs to the third level, where a
metal door led to the rooftop. When he opened it, a cold wind
blasted his face, making him squint. Soot filled the air; he could
hear coughing on the street below. The people milling about
resembled embers escaping the inferno, and the church steeple
became like a column of flame. The brightness made it diffi-
cult for his eyes to pick out the drone. But he could still hear
it, flying low, probably targeting him at that very moment. He
imagined himself appearing on a laptop screen miles away, a
white cat-shaped blob standing in a gray field.

Culdesac aimed the device in the direction of the buzzing
sound. His index finger found the awkwardly shaped trigger.
This thing he held felt like a toy. Or perhaps it was some joke
that the humans played on him. The drone operator probably
saw Culdesac on his monitor and laughed.

Culdesac pulled the trigger.

It clicked.

That was it. He pulled it again and again. Not even a rumble
or a blinking light, or any indication that the machine was doing
its job. Culdesac knew he would die in battle some day, but he
always pictured himself covered in gore, firing a pistol in one
hand, wielding a blade or a club in the other. Dying with this

malfunctioning prop from a science fiction movie did not seem fitting.

Then he saw it. His instincts were correct: the drone's nose pointed right at the station. From his vantage point, the aircraft hovered like an insect. But in truth it traveled faster than any bird, and could fire again at any moment.

Culdesac walked over to the edge of the roof and planted his foot on the ledge, as if any of that would make a difference. He lined up the flying monster in his sights and clicked away until his finger stiffened into a single brittle bone.

A light blinked from the side of the drone, like a starburst. The flash illuminated the trees below it. The drone had fired. By the time the sound reached Culdesac, he would be vaporized. A calm oozed down his body. His jaw unclenched and hung loose in his mouth. His tail went limp, his shoulders slumped.

The world brightened. He was in the steeple again, enveloped in the smell of coffee so strong it made his whiskers flutter. Nox sat beside him, leaning her head on his shoulder as they reclined under a blue sky, with the green valley splitting open beneath it. Another life, a path he could not take. Nox mumbled to him in the language of his people, growling his name in the old tongue. She said, *Find me here. Be here with me.* He sank into her, their bodies fitting together, her tail wrapping around his waist, with the tip brushing his face. Perhaps the Queen led him this far to give him this brief feeling of joy, this forbidden escape that he could never contemplate in his waking moments.

He snapped out of it when the whistling of the rocket became a scream. With a mere blink, Culdesac stood on the rooftop again. The missile streaked overhead in a great roar that knocked him over. The jet trail hung over the police station. As he tried to follow the missile's path, he saw the exhaust port glowing yellow before burning out. Seconds later, the drone passed overhead, so low he thought he could touch one of its fins. A great wind followed it as the machine pitched hard to the left. With its rear propeller switched off, the drone sank and sank until it disappeared into the valley. In the scant moonlight, Culdesac saw several trees snap at their base as the machine collided with them. Wood cracked and splintered before going silent. The forest swallowed the bird of prey.

Culdesac knelt there, propping himself on the jamming device as he gathered his thoughts. The tiny green light flickered and then faded out.

CHAPTER SIX
THE SHELL GIVES WAY

THE ACRID SMELL of smoke lingered over the town, resisting the pull of the wind. It was better than the smell of death, but both odors had a habit of sticking to the fur, between the toes, warning of things to come.

Amidst the shouting outside the police station, Culdesac returned the ray gun to its crate and closed the lid. With the battery dead, the device was useless. Culdesac assured himself that a second drone strike was unlikely. Then again, so was the first.

In the lobby, the wounded lined up for treatment from Tiberius. He told the civilians that those willing to endure a stitching without a painkiller would move to the front of the line. Taking him up on the offer, a badger nonetheless cursed Tiberius's mother each time the cat fastened a stitch on his leg. "Go ahead," Tiberius told him. "Never met her."

Outside, Mort(e) gave Culdesac a quick summary. One casualty: Seljuk. The fire burned too hot to retrieve the body, a fact that angered Culdesac even more than the cat's death. Nearly a year earlier, he broke Seljuk's nose while training him for hand-to-hand combat. The cat bounced right up, snorted the blood and snot out of his nostrils, and kept fighting. The other soldiers cheered for their wounded comrade. None of that toughness did him any good against a human death machine launched from afar by cowards.

"That's not all," Mort(e) said. "We're missing one civilian."

It was Maynard, the obnoxious Chihuahua. Culdesac asked if the dog was inside the Royal Inn, but Mort(e) said no. He slipped away in the confusion.

"Maybe his sister knows why," Culdesac said.

"She has already been detained." They kept her in the kitchen of the Mexican restaurant on Booth Street, away from the others.

Culdesac ordered Mort(e) to take two soldiers, find the drone, and rip out its computer brain before the humans salvaged it. Maybe they could use the computer to find a more reliable way to disable the drones. Though the missile might prove useful as well, it flew too far away for them to find before daybreak. Let the humans take the risk of trying to retrieve it. With any luck, they would blow themselves up in the process.

After Mort(e) left, Culdesac went to the restaurant. The glass door was open, and a few candles flickered inside. In the main dining area, several of the tables and chairs had tumbled to the floor. The cash register rested on its side, its drawer hanging out like a tongue. Behind it, Rookie, one of his foot soldiers, stood in the doorway to the kitchen. Rookie had mostly white fur, with a patch of brown and black running from his forehead to his tail. A claw mark on his shoulder left a hairless strip of flesh, a sure sign that he was a stray before the Change. He chose his name because, in his words, he liked it when people under-estimated him, treated him like he didn't know what he was doing. He knew all right.

"She's in here, sir," Rookie said. Culdesac stepped into the kitchen, where Nox sat on a milk crate beside the walk-in refrig-erator. She wore a black leather vest, fashioned from a jacket with the sleeves cut off. Nox seemed neither surprised nor relieved to see him.

"Wait outside," Culdesac said.

After Rookie closed the door, Culdesac waited in silence for Nox to speak. But she would not budge. She licked her lips once, and her ears twitched at the sounds coming from the street.

"I'm sorry about the Royal Inn," he said at last.

"I'm sorry about your soldier. I asked him if he needed company for the evening, but he said he was on duty. Thought you should know."

"I appreciate that."

Another awkward pause. She must have known why he was there.

"Are you going to bribe me, or threaten me?" she asked.

"I'm happy to start with bribery."

"I told the others, Captain. I don't know where my brother went. I'm sorry."

Culdesac paced the floor. He absently wandered to an oven with a glass window, where skinned chickens had once roasted on metal spits.

"Do you remember when I said that I speak to the Queen?" he asked, gripping the plastic handle of the spit.

"Yes."

"Do you know what that means?"

"I've heard of it. You use a device to communicate with the ants."

"That's right. And that means that I know some things that most people don't."

Her eyes widened and her whiskers slanted downward.

"I know that there is a human offensive on its way here. General Fitzpatrick is on the move again. I also know that there is an elite unit of Alpha soldiers lurking in the forest. If your brother is out there, he's going to get caught in the middle. The Alphas will make no distinction between human and animal. Every living thing in their path will be destroyed. Even if your brother is captured by the humans, the ants will wipe them all out. Just to be sure."

Nox looked at the floor.

"Have you ever seen Alphas on the hunt before?" Culdesac asked. "They surround their prey. They don't make a sound. They don't waste any time. They don't fight over scraps. And they leave nothing behind, not even a drop of blood. It's beautiful."

Nox swallowed. Nervously, she licked her paw and ran it over her face like a pet. "He's at his master's old place," she said.

"Why?"

"He thought he'd be safe there. When you showed up, he wanted to hide in his old dog house because he knew there'd be trouble."

"Where is this place?"

"I'll show you."

"Tell me."

"I'll *show* you."

Culdesac sighed. "He's going to die out there. You're not in a position to negotiate."

"I don't want you sending your meathead soldiers. They'll shoot him."

"So will I if he doesn't cooperate."

"No. He respects you. He'll listen."

"He called me a choke-dick earlier today," Culdesac said, realizing he sounded like a child tattling on someone.

Nox folded her hands, pleading like a human penitent. "Please, try to understand, he's been through a lot. I know you're strong. He isn't. And he acts the way he does so he can fake it."

Culdesac watched her, this former house pet that tempted him in what he thought would be the final moments in his life. The Queen did not prepare him for this. Maybe she didn't know. No, that wasn't right. The Queen saw everything. She wanted him to make a choice without her. She tested him.

"How far is it?" he asked.

"Not far."

THE NOISE IN the town square receded into the distance as Culdesac and Nox made their way into the deserted part of Milton. There, the grass on the lawns grew waist-high, and the light barely penetrated the trees. With each block they passed, the houses grew smaller, more jammed together until they formed neat brick rows, nearly identical. These gave way to abandoned lots squared off by rusty chain link fences. Beyond that, the factory, its painted logo washed away by the wind and the sun. At the edge of the forest lay the junkyard, where the abandoned vehicles of Milton rusted and melted into the earth. Stale rainwater formed puddles in the tire tracks. Under the sliver of moon, the cars and trucks resembled eerie mountain ranges, an alien landscape from some science fiction comic book. Culdesac did not belong here, out in the wilderness with some stranger. The Queen let him go off on his own. As soon as he let go of the tether that connected them, the predictable life he led since the Change blurred into this dream world.

Part of him liked it—the part of him that the Change was supposed to destroy.

"This is it," Nox whispered.

She pointed to a wooden sign fastened to the gate.

PAULIE'S SALVAGE, STORAGE & RENTAL
"NO QUESTIONS ASKED!"

"Have you been here before?" he asked.

"Only once. After we chased the humans away. I've never been inside."

In the center of the lot, a garage stood among the rows of cars, like a castle surrounded by trenches and battlements. Culdesac and Nox looked at each other once more before entering. The gates clicked shut behind them. The two cats slinked along the car bumpers and open trunks. As they drew closer, Nox explained that when Paulie went into the nursing home, his son took over the family business. Culdesac shushed her when he noticed a light emanating from above the vehicles. He crouched behind an old taxicab and peered around the side. Near the front of the parking lot, an orange Volkswagen sat on a flatbed truck, its headlights switched on and pointing directly into the forest. Culdesac drew his gun.

The Volkswagen and the flatbed cabin appeared to be empty. Someone switched on the lights and then walked away. He supposed that he could smash them out, but they had already made enough noise.

The garage was constructed of cinder blocks coated with chipped powder-blue paint. The main doors were closed, but the side entrance opened with a simple turn of the knob. Culdesac glanced at Nox, who waved him on. He put his hand up to indicate that he wanted her to wait outside. No point in both of them getting trapped. Leading with the barrel of his gun, Culdesac stepped inside and swept the room. When his eyes readjusted to the darkness, he saw nothing out of the ordinary. A metal desk stood in the corner, covered in invoices and other paperwork. On a nearby table, the mechanics left behind wrenches, hammers, drills. A Milton Police paddy wagon was parked near the main doors.

Culdesac slid along the wall to see what lurked behind the

truck. There, in the corner, Maynard the pain-in-the-ass Chihuahua sat in a round dog bed, with his wheelchair beside him. On the seat of the chair, an ashtray held a freshly stubbed cigarette. Next to that: a bottle of bourbon, nearly empty.

Though made for a pet, the bed barely contained Maynard's girth. While his paralyzed legs hung over the sides, Maynard's decidedly useful hands held a revolver, shakily pointed at Culdesac. Clearly nervous, the dog panted, his bulging eyes glistening in the scant light.

"If that was loaded, you would have shot me by now," Culdesac said.

Maynard set the gun on the ground and belched. "Maybe you should shoot me."

"I've considered it."

"Might as well," Maynard slurred. "You take us away from our home, leave us for dead."

Having heard the voices, Nox stepped inside the garage and raced to her brother, nearly knocking Culdesac over. She wrapped her arms around the dog's skinny neck, but then recoiled at the smell of liquor.

"I told you not to come here," she said. When his head rolled a bit on his shoulders, she shook him awake again. "Do you hear me? What's wrong with you?"

"Needed to see it again."

"We talked about this. You told me—"

"I found Greta," Maynard said. "She's still here."

Maynard nodded toward the manager's office. Nox let go of him and walked over to the door.

"Who's Greta?" Culdesac asked.

"Paulie's son Frank had a . . . cock-a," Maynard said, hiccupping.

"A what?"

Behind him, Nox turned the doorknob and creaked open the door.

"A fucking . . . cock-a," Maynard stammered. "A bird. A cock-a-something."

"Cockatoo?"

"Yeah. I used to bark at her all day. I wanted to know why she wouldn't come out of her cage and play with me."

Nox screamed.

"I think she was laughing at me," Maynard said, ignoring the interruption.

Culdesac followed the noise. A putrid smell leaked from the room. Inside, bird feathers covered the floor, the computer monitor, the desk, the shelves, the filing cabinets. A few even drifted onto the motionless blades of the ceiling fan.

In the corner, a birdcage lay on the floor, tipped over, its metal bars twisted and bent. Inside, the remains of Greta hardened and calcified. Frank abandoned the garage without her. As a final punishment for her terrible luck in life, Greta grew in size while still in her prison. She was not stuck inside the cage so much as wrapped in it, the bars cutting into her flesh. Judging from her broken wings, she tried to smash her way out, probably after going insane shouting for help. In a rage, she ripped out most of her feathers, leaving the scaly, pink skin exposed. Dried blood stained her chipped beak. Her left claw had been gnawed to a stump, the half-chewed bones and nails nearly indistinguishable from the feces scattered about. Culdesac noticed the newspaper lining the floor of the cage. The top story mentioned the wall of fire that the humans used to hold off the ant infestation in Central America, meaning that the paper came out mere days before the first confirmed Alpha attack.

Nox tried to squelch her sobbing, but it did no good. Culdesac placed his hand on the back of her neck and felt the choking sound in her throat. She turned and rested her furry face on his shoulder.

"Maynard blames himself," she said. "We should have checked on her. Made sure she got out."

"It's nobody's fault."

"Isn't it?" she asked, stepping away from him. "How many people died like this? How many people did the Queen leave behind?"

"The *humans* put her in a cage. Not the Queen."

"The humans at least fed her!"

Culdesac could not think of anything to say. Nox had a point: How many people perished in their cages, finally cognizant of their slavish existence and yet powerless to do a thing about it? This bird never gave herself a proper name, never saw others like her rise up and fight. The Queen saw everything, including this, and she decided to move forward anyway.

"When I came up with the idea for the coffee shop," Nox said, "I thought I was doing my part to fix all of this."

It was a stupid thing to say. A *coffee* shop, making things better. But Culdesac knew enough about people to keep this thought to himself. He could not hide his feelings from Hymenoptera Unus, who hovered over him day and night, despite the distance between them. But he could conceal things from this cat who stood right in front of him, who spoke to him face to face.

"You joined the army to help people, right?" she asked.

"Yes." He lied, but it felt true because it was what she needed to hear.

"I mean, that's what we're supposed to do now," she said. "We have to reach out to everyone. Save as many as we can."

Outside, someone opened the gate to the junkyard. The grinding metal echoed among the dead cars. Nox heard it, too.

They hurried into the garage, where Maynard nervously peered out the window from his wheelchair.

The side door was cracked open. Culdesac crept to it and peeked outside.

Six humans entered the property, heading down the main driveway, about one hundred fifty meters away. Each wore night-vision goggles and camouflage gear—as if that made a difference with felines. Culdesac spotted grenades dangling from their front pockets. These were no farmers. Most likely, they operated the drone from earlier that evening.

Instinctively, Culdesac patted his sidearm.

"How many bullets do you have?" Nox whispered.

"Doesn't matter. These noisemakers will get you killed in a situation like this."

"We should surrender," Maynard said, more alert now. "There are six of them."

"Better than seven."

"Should we wait here?" Nox asked.

"We'll be surrounded. Then six turns into twelve."

"So what then?" Maynard said.

"We go hunting."

Oh, Culdesac missed the hunt.

"I can't hunt," Maynard said.

"You're bait," Culdesac said. "That's all I need from you."

"Am *I* bait?" Nox asked.

Culdesac smiled. "You're a decoy."

"What's the difference?"

"A decoy is actually useful."

Nox giggled, then seemed embarrassed for doing so.

"Fuck you, bobcat," Maynard said.

"Fuck *you*. It's *your* fault we're in this mess."

"I didn't ask you to come looking for me."

"Stay there and keep quiet," Culdesac said. "And if I hear you talk about surrender one more time, I'll twist your head off your shoulders. Boil the flesh, wear the skull like a necklace."

The dog turned to his sister for support, but she gave him a look that Culdesac recognized. It said *shut up*.

Outside, the humans drew closer. Culdesac could not smell them yet, but the clumsy noise of their boots and their breath gave them away, as always, as if they *wanted* him to find them and kill them.

IF TIME ALLOWED, Culdesac would have tried to explain to Nox and Maynard the art of war. After all, even the dimmest among the animals—the livestock and beasts of burden—could figure it out, so long as they stopped being afraid, and accepted that all living things, animal and human, were subject to the laws of physics, natural selection, and their own narrow view of the world.

What most civilians failed to understand about the art of war was that the enemy, if given enough time, always handed over the keys to victory—provided that one is keen enough to notice. On this evening, the humans planned an ambush. But they stampeded into the unknown, noisy, overconfident, thereby negating their numerical advantage. The unnatural terrain of this metal graveyard provided the same kind of battlefield that Culdesac had endured for years, both as a kitten struggling to survive, and as a soldier in the greatest empire the world had ever known. Here, amidst the slim corridors and shoe-swallowing mud puddles, one stubborn bastard of a bobcat could hold off an army. The junkyard would funnel the enemy, close off his avenue of escape, and provide cover to regroup. The graveyard in Milton would need some fresh dirt before sunrise.

Flat on his stomach, Culdesac watched from underneath a station wagon that stood on cinder blocks. From there, he saw the humans make their first mistake, one that he anticipated: at an intersection in the junk piles, two of the soldiers broke off to check the southern end of the lot. A sound move on familiar ground, but very risky here. Rather than conserving their impregnable strength, the humans spread themselves thin. In situations like this, humans tended to fortify their position in as many places as possible, which merely dulled their sharp points and created more weak ones.

Culdesac crawled beneath the vehicle, slinking through a trench filled with brackish water, so cold that it burned. He spotted the two soldiers' boots tromping along the tire tracks. One of them veered off to the side to lift the tarp from the rear of a pickup. The other crouched to check under the car bumpers. Culdesac would strike them first. That was how it worked. Attack the weakness, keep hitting until the enemy can no longer hold the middle, until every exposed surface becomes a weak spot. The shell gives way to tender flesh.

Culdesac waited between a school bus and a minivan. When the soldier poked his head into that space, Culdesac snatched the goggles, wrenched them upward, and slashed the man's throat. Barely breathing, the man consented to being dragged to the driver's side of the bus. Culdesac flopped the body over the seat, climbed the hood of the nearest car, and bounded over the skeleton of a delivery van. The man's partner arrived, whispering his name: "Blake! *Blake!*" Maybe he noticed the pin missing from poor Blake's hand grenade. Or maybe he didn't. The grenade exploded regardless, shattering the tense silence. Shards of glass and shrapnel and pieces of the two men ascended into the sky and then returned to the earth.

The other soldiers shouted, not to convey information so much as to reassert some illusion of control over the situation.

"Take cover!" someone said.

"They're firing!"

"Blake!"

The scent of blood overwhelmed the rust and the dirt. That, along with the growing racket, the confused voices, made Culdesac's heart race, even as everything around him slowed down.

He mounted another vehicle and doubled back. The humans heard him coming. Someone shouted for the others to shut up and listen. Culdesac saw one of the men standing far from the group, hesitant to investigate whatever happened to Blake.

Another weak spot.

Culdesac leapt from the roof of a Suburban and landed feet first on the man's shoulders, driving him into the dirt and collapsing the ribs onto the lungs and heart. As Culdesac rolled for cover behind the other row of vehicles, the soldier vomited blood in a fit of violent coughing.

The three soldiers who remained saw this too late. They fired blindly, igniting the junkyard with the flashpoints of their rifles. Bullets punctured the car doors and ruptured the windshields. Something whizzed by Culdesac's ears as he dove behind an old police car. Kneeling, he patted his fur, checking for wounds that he could not feel in this heightened state. His hand came up dry.

The volley of bullets faded out. A few pieces of glass and other debris fell to the ground. Then, silence.

Right on cue, the trash truck parked near the garage started its engine. It was the decoy. Nox would turn the key as soon as she heard the first hail of gunfire. Culdesac saw the truck's only functioning headlight switch on. Without a driver, the vehicle rolled on an incline, headed toward the southern gate. Its bumper grazed a convertible, then grinded along the side of a Camaro. Gaining speed, the metal monster swerved and then careened into a tow truck before coming to a halt, its driver-side door pinned shut. The engine continued to run. Over the noise, Culdesac tried to listen for the sound of footsteps. Sure enough, one of the three humans set out to investigate, weakening what remained of the pack once again. So predictable, these humans. They probably communicated all of this with their ridiculous hand signals, as if that would keep things too quiet for a bobcat to hear.

That left only two soldiers coming his way. Culdesac almost felt bad for them when they emerged from a row of cars, into the open, their goggles jouncing on their pink, clean-shaven faces. Young men, full of opportunity before the war began. As they approached the police car, Culdesac opened a pouch on his belt and pulled out one of the road flares he swiped from the garage. He popped off the white cap and placed the red tube into his teeth. The soldiers stopped in their tracks. Culdesac tossed the cap over his shoulder. It landed on the roof of a car. As the soldiers turned to the sound, Culdesac sprung from his position and charged the nearest man. Before the soldier could swing his rifle to fire, Culdesac grabbed the stock with both hands and used it to smash the man in the face, breaking his goggles. Twisting the rifle strap, he then swung the man around to use him as a human shield. Culdesac pulled the flare from his mouth and struck it against the soldier's cheek, leaving a blackened welt across the jawbone. The flare ignited, its angry red fire revealing the blood streaming from the human's mouth and eye sockets. Culdesac jabbed the flame at the second soldier's goggles, blinding him. As the man staggered, Culdesac hooked his claws around his collar and pulled him down hard into his knee, splintering the nose and teeth. The soldier crumpled, either dead or unconscious. Culdesac lifted the first man and then slammed him into the dirt, the body limp and compliant.

"No!" he heard Nox scream. Culdesac tried to place the sound—it came from the truck. In his delirium of bloodlust and violence, he quickly put it together. Nox did not merely start the engine and put the truck in neutral. She tried to drive it for some reason.

"Don't shoot!" she said.

And now she was trapped.

Culdesac let go of the soldier and bolted toward the sound, using all four limbs to vault over the rows of cars. In her voice, Culdesac heard his wounded brother pleading for mercy as the hunters overtook him. He heard his mother calling for him. He could not save them. The past swallowed them up. But this was the ever-flowing present, the river that emptied into an infinite number of streams. He could change the path of this current whenever he chose.

The human stood near the trash truck, aiming his rifle at the demon hurtling toward him. Culdesac saw the man take a step backward. The soldier was afraid at the very moment he needed to breathe and aim and fire. If only he took a step forward to throw Culdesac off his stride. If only he knew the game.

The muzzle flash illuminated the ground at the man's feet, but the rounds sailed over Culdesac's ears. Culdesac launched from the roof of a car and landed in the mud, his feet tearing out wet clumps earth. When he got close enough, Culdesac placed all of his weight into the heel of his hand as he drove it into the man's jaw, pitching him into the truck. The helmet collided with the steel. The man's teeth clacked shut. The soldier spit one out in a miasma of blood and saliva.

Culdesac raked his claws on the human's chest, opening a void in the man's insides that glistened even in the dark. Hot blood erupted from the wound, drenching Culdesac's arm. The man dropped to his knees and keeled over, letting out a final moan. But it was not enough for Culdesac. He pinned the man in the dirt and kept slashing. Left, right, left, right, left, right. The cloth streamed outward from the corpse in sopping wet ribbons. The skin tore away, exposing the rib cage. Culdesac's nails grew warm from the blood and the friction. On one side, the blood sprayed several feet from the corpse. On the other, the blood splashed as high as the top of the truck, as if thrown with buckets. When Culdesac stopped slashing and realized how far he dispersed the human's remains, he finally breathed again. The stale air vacated his lungs. His drenched hands fell to his sides.

As the world returned to normal speed, and his senses reset, he detected a now-familiar scent emanating from what remained of the man. It was that damned coffee again, the stuff Nox swore the humans could not do without. It may have mingled with his bloodstream, or spilled from some vessel on his person. With little energy left to investigate, Culdesac considered the possibility that he simply imagined the scent.

The passenger door of the truck popped open. Maynard slid out, hands first, his paralyzed legs dragging behind him. His eyes bulged at the sight of the eviscerated human. Nox followed. She saw Culdesac, straddling the husk of the soldier. Her blank expression conveyed neither shock nor grief, only a grim acceptance of things, how they were and how they would always be. She was no soldier, but she had seen enough of this world to know. Right and wrong, good and bad—all meaningless concepts in the war with no name. Only luck kept her from ending up like this human.

"You killed them," Maynard said. His surprise suggested that this was a question.

"They killed themselves," Culdesac said.

The dog trembled. With an aching tenderness, Nox knelt beside her brother, held his hand, and rested her cheek on the crown of his head, folding his pointy ears underneath. The three remained in that position until the last hints of the coffee scent faded away.

CHAPTER SEVEN
THE UNDERGROUND RAILROAD

HEY WALKED UNDER pink clouds, the last sunrise they would see in Milton. Culdesac pushed Maynard's wheelchair while Nox strolled beside him. Ambling along the sidewalk on South Booth Street, they must have resembled some twisted family: a lovely mother, a father who was not attractive enough for her, and their mutant offspring who probably wasn't even his.

Nox and Maynard took turns explaining their rationale for driving the truck rather than simply starting the ignition and rolling it down the hill, like Culdesac had asked.

"I know how to drive!" Nox said. Culdesac told her to keep her voice down. There could still be humans out there. And his own soldiers might mistake them for the enemy.

"I've seen her drive," Maynard said. "She used the nursing home bus until it ran out of gas." After the initial uprising, with the town divided between human and animal, the bus served as an ambulance, transporting the wounded to a safe zone.

"But why drive the truck?" Culdesac asked.

"I told you!" Nox whined. "I thought I could drive it through the gate. But it hit a bump and it swerved and—"

"I talked her into it," Maynard said. "I didn't want to get stuck there as bait."

Culdesac sighed.

"We're not all super-warriors like you, dickhead," Maynard said. "Besides, you may have saved our lives, but we saved yours too. We drew their fire, like you said."

Nox reminded Maynard that he was the one who got them into this mess.

"No, *he* got us into this mess!" Maynard said. "We didn't have drone strikes until the Red Sphinx showed up. Now we've got a big fucking bull's eye on our backs."

Nox looked to Culdesac for a reaction. He would not give her one, and instead continued to roll the chair as though he barely heard any of this.

"Drone strikes," Culdesac mused. "And a sniper who coated himself with Vaseline. And an elite unit of soldiers. The humans were willing to use some of their best resources on this town. Any guesses as to why?"

"I told you already," Maynard said. "We have access to the river, access to the bridge. You don't have to be Napoleon to figure it out."

"The humans would have blown up the bridge if we hadn't stopped them," Nox added.

"And after you fought them off the first time," Culdesac said. "Did you pursue them into the woods? Did you try to finish them off?"

"We chased them. The ones we cornered committed suicide rather than be caught. They must know by now what the Queen does with prisoners."

Ah, yes. Human prisoners were often sent to the Island, where they would be test subjects in the race to find a cure for EMSAH. Or simply because it amused the Queen.

"How did the rest get away?" Culdesac asked.

"We get it," Maynard said. "The Red Sphinx wouldn't have let them escape. We tried, okay? We held the town for you. You're welcome."

"They escaped from your territory. Your people knew the terrain."

Nox and Maynard looked at one another again. They didn't even try to hide it.

"The humans have gotten smarter," Nox said. "You must have seen it. They've even learned to mask their scent."

Culdesac recalled the empty canister he found in the woods, the one filled with urine that led him in the wrong direction. But the human penchant for cleverness had run its course. Soon, they would find themselves so overwhelmed that no diversion would save them.

"We've gotten smarter, too," Culdesac said.

They walked for a while in silence. All three of them still needed to process what had happened, and what lay ahead. Within hours, most likely, the humans would level this town. Having survived for so long with no place to call home, Culdesac did not understand this attachment to a single location. But it began to make sense now, with both the animals and the humans willing to die for it. The land stayed in place while the people grew old and passed on. The buildings and the roads and the rivers outlasted flesh. They provided a safe haven from the cruelty of mortality. It was no wonder how far people would go to protect it.

As they approached the intersection of Main and Booth, Nox walked close beside him. Unwilling to hold his hand—probably because Maynard was right there—she let her furry tail wrap around his waist until its warmth radiated up his spine.

MORT(E) DID NOT look happy when Culdesac arrived. Neither did anyone else. The civilians stood in two ragged lines, stretching outward from the town square. Each of them held what they could carry. Some of them wore backpacks, while others hugged pillowcases full of their belongings. A few old ones sat in wheelchairs, and one elderly cat squatted in a wheelbarrow. The people had a desperate smell about them. This was the moment that would either make them stronger or destroy them. Some day, the intelligent ones among them would be grateful for the experience.

Nearby, members of the Red Sphinx stood in formation, exhausted but focused on the task at hand. In the morning light, the charred remains of the Royal Inn blotted the neighborhood, its black stain oozing as far as the sidewalk.

"Captain," Nox said. "Let me see my Inn one more time before we leave. Please."

"You'll have to hear about it all the way to the Pharaohs if you don't," Maynard said.

Culdesac agreed. As Nox jogged up Main Street, Culdesac pointed to Dread, who stood in formation with the others. Dread immediately understood that he should follow her.

Mort(e) approached and saluted impatiently. "Sir, may I speak with you in private?"

"No need," Culdesac said. "Say what you have to say."

Mort(e) glanced at the Chihuahua and continued. "The drone computer is secure. But…may I ask where you went?"

His tone suggested that Culdesac made a mistake. Mort(e) was out of line talking like this, but Culdesac could hardly blame him.

"I saw an opportunity to kill some humans, and I took it," Culdesac said.

"But there was no one in command."

"Striker was the ranking officer. And besides, it was worth it."

"How?" Mort(e) raised his voice enough for everyone to hear. Maynard sunk in his chair.

"I'll show you. Get the Texan to bring over her barbecue supplies."

Mort(e) blinked at the non-sequitur. "Barbecue?"

"Just do it."

"Yes, sir."

Mort(e) marched over to the formation and yanked Texan out of line. He gestured to her backpack. She unzipped it and began fishing around inside. Meanwhile, Culdesac continued to roll Maynard in the direction of the fountain.

"Smart mouth on that one," the dog said.

"That's why I promoted him."

"Yeah, but you can't tolerate that kind of back talk. The army can't work like that. You need to slap these fuckers around when they get rowdy. Otherwise, it's chaos."

Culdesac halted at the fountain and spun the chair around. He crouched and grinned at Maynard, baring his fangs in all their glory.

"We're not the army. We're the Red Sphinx. 'Aim true. Stay on the hunt.'"

"Sir!" Mort(e) said from behind him.

Texan held her bag open. "I have the supplies you requested," she said.

"Give me the lighter fluid."

As soon as she handed over the metal tin, Culdesac removed the plastic cap from the nozzle and sprayed the contents onto Maynard's face, shoulders, and chest. The dog squirmed in his chair, trying to shield his eyes.

"Hey! What the fuck are you doing?" He spit out some of the fluid. The chemical stench of it engulfed them.

"Lighter," Culdesac said, holding out his palm. Texan dropped a silver Zippo in his hand. When Culdesac clicked it open, the civilians gasped. He nodded to Mort(e), who immediately aimed his rifle at the crowd to keep the people at bay. The rest of the Red Sphinx broke from their formation, creating a wall around their captain.

Culdesac rolled his thumb over the wheel. The tiny fire flared in his hand, reflected in Maynard's wet eyes. Culdesac tossed the lighter. Obeying his involuntary reflexes, the dog stupidly caught the flame in his hands. The orange fire spread to his arms, chest, and neck, making a popping sound. People in the crowd screamed. Maynard writhed in his chair, frantically patting out the flames, which only made them worse. Desperate, he rose from his seat, standing on his hind legs, and dove into the fountain like some comet touching down on the surface of the ocean. When Maynard emerged from the troubled water, Culdesac snatched him by the throat and pinned him against the stone pedestal. The fire barely left a mark, but the air was thick with the rank smell of burnt hair.

The crowd went silent as everyone tried to hear.

"The Change gave you your legs back, didn't it?" Culdesac asked. "The Queen made you whole again, and you betrayed her."

"I can explain—"

Culdesac tightened his grip. "So can I."

Culdesac turned to Mort(e) and ordered him to take five cats and meet him at the church. They had some digging to do. The rest of the soldiers would hold the civilians here.

"There's nothing in the church," Maynard gasped.

"What was it you said?" Culdesac asked. "The humans are getting better at hiding their scent?"

Maynard did not respond.

"So what's all that coffee doing in the church?" Culdesac said. "What is it hiding?"

Maynard swallowed and began to pant. He looked to the

other citizens of Milton for help, not realizing that this one move convicted all of them. Culdesac felt the muscles tense in the dog's neck. He leaned in closer.

"They're not going to help you," Culdesac said. "Look at me. When I'm done with you, you're gonna *beg* me to burn you alive."

He let go. The dog shivered in the fountain while the Red Sphinx trained their rifles on him.

"Sir!" Mort(e) called out.

Mort(e)'s soldiers gathered around a person who had fallen on the sidewalk, about two blocks from the fountain. When Culdesac arrived at the scene, he found Dread at the base of a lamppost, clutching an open wound on his ribs. A trail of blood followed him from the blast site at the Royal Inn. Mort(e) shouted for Tiberius, who came running with his first aid kit.

"She pulled a knife on me," Dread grunted. The other cats told him to relax, that he would be okay. They made room for Tiberius, who peeled away Dread's bloody hands to examine the cut.

Mort(e) whispered to Culdesac. "Should we send someone after her?"

"She won't get far," Culdesac said. "She's about to run into a wall of Alphas. I want to see what's in the church first."

"You think it's a weapon?"

"I think it's something worse."

Dread moaned as Tiberius pressed a gauze pad to his side. The doctor told the others to hold Dread's arms as he prepared the thread and needle.

"I suppose you were right about Nox, sir," Mort(e) said.

"Right." There was little point in admitting how close he had come to being wrong, and how he was almost ready to live with it. Almost.

• • •

WHEN THE SOLDIERS moved the coffee crates in the storage room of St. Michael's Church, they found the trap door leading to a hidden chamber. The same one used to smuggle contraband, from escaped slaves to alcohol. The door blended seamlessly with the floor, save for a brass handle embedded in the linoleum tile. The soldiers formed a ring around it, and gave Culdesac the honor of pulling it open.

The aperture released a stench of sweat, urine, vomit, and excrement, so powerful that not even the haze of coffee could seal it in. The cats readied their weapons. A dull radiance emanated from the opening, and a set of wooden stairs descended to a concrete floor below. Culdesac led with his pistol, his feet crunching on a fine dusting of coffee grounds. At the bottom, the chamber extended to the south, a tunnel of some sort, with brick walls on either side.

In the glow of a hanging oil lamp, humans stood on either side of the tunnel. They were mostly children, some emaciated and dead-eyed, with ragged clothes and old, rotting bandages in various places. The rest were elderly. Some sat in wheelchairs, others lay sprawled on blankets on the floor. An old man with no teeth and paper-thin flesh clutched an air tank that fed him oxygen through a tube in his nose. A little girl wearing a man's dress shirt tried to stifle her tears at the sight of these beasts entering their refuge.

From side chambers, more of them emerged, bringing their desperate scent with them, their stunned eyes too exhausted to shed any tears. The last survivors of the nursing home, stowed away until the Red Sphinx left this town behind. Nox and Maynard must have secretly brought them food. Maynard continued his charade as a paraplegic to avoid suspicion—a pointless gamble that merely delayed the inevitable. The Queen saw everything, even a hole in the ground long forgotten by humans and animals alike.

Whatever battle took place in this town was not between humans and animals, but between those who wanted to protect these humans, and those who did not. Some of the humans probably thought that they could repel the Red Sphinx long enough for their people to escape, but changing circumstances forced them to hide instead.

With Mort(e) and several other soldiers behind him, Culdesac walked deeper into the tunnel. None of these humans posed a threat. They shivered as he passed, as if his presence carried with it a chill. At the end of the tunnel, he saw a pile of broken cinder blocks and plowed earth. The passageway ended at the Royal Inn, the speakeasy from the human age. The drone strike was meant to stop anyone from finding the other entrance.

Culdesac tried to imagine the last few days for these people. The grownups probably kept the children distracted with games, with gently whispered songs and lullabies. Perhaps they prayed, or convened nightly meetings with talent shows and poetry recitals. Judging from the smell, at least one of the residents died down here, and the humans held some kind of mourning ritual despite their inability to bury the body. More than one of them must have said that they lived like animals in this cave, a thought that both angered and amused Culdesac.

"Where's Chandra?" he asked.

The humans did not even bother trying to hide her, or to stall him. The woman stepped forward, slightly shorter than the others, with enormous bags pulling at her black eyes. Gray lightning bolts streaked through her dark hair. Her threadbare nurse's scrubs clashed with her jangling gold bracelets, her necklace, and her red lipstick. Though this war aged her, shriveled her, she maintained the luxuries of jewelry and makeup while trapped here in hell.

"How do you know my name?" she asked.

"Nox. She tells me you were her favorite."

A young girl coughed. Her mother—a pale woman with a shaved head—nervously covered her mouth to silence her.

"Is Paulie here, too?" Culdesac asked.

"He died." Her voice betrayed no sadness, only a seething anger. Perhaps she tried to save his life, or to make his last hours comfortable before he expired.

"The Chihuahua told me about him," Culdesac said.

Chandra bit her lip. The red lipstick bled onto her still-perfect teeth. "Are you saying they betrayed us?"

"No. They tried to hide you."

Her lip quivered as a tear rolled off her cheek. "Then we've won. You may not see it yet. But there are others like them. They won't kill for you anymore."

She spoke with the unnerving confidence of a person who had not seen the sun in a week. These humans told themselves all kinds of stories to keep going another day. Nox loved them for it. Their words became truth, as real as anything that could be seen or touched. Nox chose this over her true destiny. And now Culdesac might never find out why.

He motioned for Mort(e) to begin rounding them up. Then he headed for the stairs.

"What will happen to us?" Chandra asked.

Culdesac stopped and cleared his throat. "Something worse than this, I'm afraid."

His second in command knew what to do from there. These humans would be detained, along with their traitorous allies outside. Some day, Culdesac would count this as a victory in the long war that lay ahead. Some day.

"Wait," Chandra said. "Nox and Maynard—are they still alive?"

Well, would you get a load of that? This slave master wanted to know if her pets survived.

"No," Culdesac said.

It felt true. He would make it true.

CHAPTER EIGHT
FAMILY

THE CAT FLED into the forest in a panic, leaving crushed grass, scuff marks in the dirt, and broken twigs in her wake. She grew more careful as she slowed, the footprints inching closer to one another. She left the trail when she could, scrabbling over boulders, slinking along felled trees. None of it would matter. She could not avoid disturbing the moss, stepping on a patch of dirt, or shedding clumps of her thick coat. But besides that, her smell dragged behind her, a mixture of coffee, fur, sex, liquor, and smoke. Which was why, instead of detouring to the barren mountains like the human had done days earlier, Nox descended straight into the valley as fast as she could, racing to the river. If she hurried, she might have time to cross—assuming she wasn't afraid of the water, like so many other housecats. Maybe then she could hide her scent and rendezvous with the humans encamped in the wilderness beyond.

Culdesac would overtake her before all that. There would be no suspense this time, no drama. He knew these woods, and Nox didn't. He knew the hunt. The hunt was life. While these woods gave him strength, they reduced her to a scared creature, a pet locked out of her master's home.

Culdesac wondered: Was Nox seeing the forest for only the

first time? After years spent as a breeder, this race through the woods may have provided the only chance to see the world before her human friends destroyed it. Spring approached, and the midday sun penetrated the thickening canopy, providing an illusion of warmth even in the breeze. New shoots and saplings poked their translucent fingers through the dirt. A beehive hummed. All of it would have been an alien landscape to Nox. If things had gone differently, he could have shown her all of this. In a way, that was exactly what he was doing.

The scent grew stronger at a steep point on the trail, where a boulder poked out of the earth, forming a small cliff. In a hurry to get around it, Nox tried to slide down the rock face, only to skin a knee or an elbow. Culdesac scaled it on all fours, his nose leading the way to the tiny wet skid mark, sticky with her blood. He licked it, and then rolled his tongue along the roof of his mouth. She was a part of him now, activating all of his senses. A few feet away, a divot in the sparse patch of grass suggested that she rested here, nursing her wound. Culdesac crept over to the spot, hovered above it, letting her smell drift onto him, into him. She would never know how her scent conjured his mother's purring, his brother's growling. When he closed his eyes, he saw the female bobcat from years earlier, looking away from him while he took what he wanted. Ashamed but not defeated. And that memory dissolved, as it always did, into the image of the female's carcass, with Murmur standing over it, his mouth and claws painted bright red.

If he lingered too long in the memory, the female bobcat would turn into Nox.

Culdesac moved on. With no supplies, Nox would be drawn to sources of food or water. Culdesac found signs of her presence near a stagnant pond. Indentations in the mud showed that she knelt down to take a drink, her throat as dry as sandpaper.

Taking a cue from the humans, she then urinated in the pond in the hopes it would disperse the scent. It failed—Culdesac caught a trace of it in the breeze. Though refreshed, Nox nevertheless grew exhausted. The footprints revealed a staggering gait, delirious. Culdesac noticed a claw mark on a tree and wondered if she held onto it for support before sliding off. It would not be long now.

A rustling in the trees to the east. A rumbling in the earth. Culdesac hid behind a tree and watched the leaves shake loose and drift to the ground. Three enormous black pods emerged, Alpha soldiers on patrol. They were part of the Queen's trap for the humans, a pincer movement that would shear off the enemy's head. Culdesac rose from his hiding spot and held out his hands. The creatures approached and probed him with their antennae. The smaller ones scurried about on the exoskeletons, forming odd symmetrical patterns as they recognized this ally in the war. Though they could not communicate directly, these animals of different species nevertheless shared a common goal, a common enemy. On the hunt, instinct and empathy replaced reason and language. Still, Culdesac regretted leaving the translator behind. He wanted to hear the Queen's voice. He wanted her to guide him through this, to assure him that she had foreseen this, and that all of it served a greater good. But then he remembered: she wanted him to face this alone, as a sentient being rather than a mere animal, or a soldier following orders. He understood now.

His energy restored, Culdesac bounded through the forest with his sisters. He was one of them, a part of a whole that hunted as a single organism. No talk, no fear, no regret—a feeling of freedom that he never experienced while prowling the forest with Murmur. Culdesac would never understand why the animals in Milton would reject this gift from the Queen. He blamed the humans. Their corruption spread so far, even into the hearts of the very people they enslaved.

Culdesac and the Alphas found Nox a mere quarter of a mile from the river. She heard them coming. Knowing that she would not make it, she collapsed in a clearing, her back rising with each breath, her tail flat beside her. A nearby tree bore her claw marks, but she gave up on trying to climb. It was no use.

Culdesac made it to her first. When the Alphas surrounded them, he raised his hands. One by one, the sisters skidded to a halt and lifted their antennae. They knew that he needed a minute. The Queen must have told them.

Nox gathered herself, got to her feet. A patch of mud stuck to her belly. The fur on her knee tangled around a wet scab. Exhausted and emaciated, she resembled so many of his people in the days leading up to the Change.

"What happened to the town?" she asked.

"Quarantine."

"Did the people make it out?"

Instead of lying to her, Culdesac merely stared until she understood.

"It's all gone," she whispered. Shaking, she took a few steps away from him. She tripped on a root and clutched a tree to steady herself.

"Do you have any idea why I had to do it? Those humans took care of us. We were a family."

"Family," he sneered. "They used you. You were their slaves."

"It might be simple for you. It's not simple for me."

"It's simple for me because I've seen what they can do."

"Well, I've seen what *you* can do. I've seen what the Colony did to you."

One of the Alphas stirred. They would not stand still for long, no matter how much the Queen favored this bobcat.

"What the Colony did to me," he began. "What the *Queen* did, was set me free."

"If you're free, then prove it. Let me go."

Culdesac tilted his head.

"Or come with me," she said. "The Colony is going to lose this war. And then we'll rebuild. Animals and humans together. We don't have to fight anymore. It'll be different."

He could picture it: The cannons and tanks going silent, sitting dormant in the fields and on the streets. Animals and humans plowing a freshly tilled garden, laughing, singing. Nox standing by his side, her arm around his shoulders. Children chasing one another, giggling. The image came though in blinding primary colors, like some human-made poster. This was his last chance at whatever life the humans offered. And rather than feeling it slide off of him like some great weight, he simply let it slip from his hand and drop into the abyss.

"I *am* free," he said. "This is my family."

He turned his back on her. As he left the clearing, the Alphas rushed in. He heard clawing and scraping behind him as he walked deeper into the forest. But Nox did not make a sound.

CHAPTER NINE
THE EMBERS

ULDESAC FOUND THE Red Sphinx at the entrance to the caves at the Pharaohs. Uzi stood guard and gave him a salute when he got close enough. Culdesac was too tired to reciprocate. She knew him well enough to leave any questions for the morning. Instead, she pointed to the cave that she reserved for him, near the top of the hill.

After their long journey, most of the soldiers had already retired for the day, though Culdesac spotted a few pairs of eyes staring out from the caves. Striker and Gai Den nodded to him as they cleaned their guns. Dread leaned on a boulder picking at the fresh stitches in his side. Logan, still on chow duty, collected the mobile mess kit, making sure to not bang the pots and pans together too loudly. All in all, these caves felt more natural than the supposed comforts of the human village. The Red Sphinx slept in the wilderness, not in beds with fluffy pillows. Even better: they were on their own again, free from watching over civilians who still wanted to be pets. They would have some new stories from the whorehouse to replace their old ones, and to tide them over until they came across the next settlement.

By then, the sunset formed a yellow ribbon along the hills to the west. To the north, a column of smoke marked the location of Milton—what was left of it. Fires burned in the surrounding forest. The humans walked right into the Queen's trap. Sweeping into Milton, they encountered a newly established clutch of Alpha soldiers. For months, the humans poked at the nest, only to discover a torrent of ants gushing out, drowning the forest. As night crept in, the explosions blinked on the horizon, followed by a thud seconds later. *Bah-boom. Bah-boom.* Like waves crashing on sharp rocks.

Near the entrance to his cave, Culdesac found Tiberius and Mort(e) sitting on two wooden crates, with a third crate between them serving as a table. As he expected, the logo for Darby Coffee, Ltd appeared on the side, with its image of a circular map of the world. Next to it, a kettle sat on the red-hot ashes of a dying fire, with steam rising from its spout. The two cats leaned on their elbows, each holding a set of playing cards in their hands. They used cat treats for chips. Tiberius showed a pair of kings. Mort(e) drew two more cards, but did not seem thrilled with the replacements. When they saw him approaching, they slapped their cards on the makeshift table and saluted him. He told them to relax, and to continue with their game.

"Can we deal you in, Captain?" Tiberius asked.

"I don't like poker."

"Neither do I," Mort(e) said. He spread his cards out, revealing a diamond, a heart, a club, and two spades.

"Wait, you were supposed to give me a chance to throw in," Tiberius said.

"I wasn't going to win. This game has nothing to do with skill. It's all based on the cards you draw."

"It's about bluffing. Even if you have a bad hand, you can bluff me into folding."

"It's a stupid game."

They went back and forth, with Tiberius haranguing

Mort(e) about quitting too soon. "It's *not* a stupid game!" he said. "It's about life! You play the cards you've been dealt!"

"Socks, give it a rest," Culdesac said. That usually shut him up.

The kettle began to whistle. Tiberius took it from the embers and set it on the grass. Mort(e) pulled two mugs from his rucksack, along with a metal strainer. On the other side of the crate, Culdesac noticed a bowl with a smooth rock inside, filled with freshly ground coffee.

"Did you bring the crates so you can brew some of this stuff?" Culdesac asked.

"We wanted to try it, yes," Tiberius said. He scooped the grounds with the strainer. Mort(e) poured the hot water through it and into the mugs.

"You won't like it," Culdesac said.

"I wanted to try it anyway. Besides, we thought *you* liked it."

Culdesac could no longer remember if he did nor did not. "It'll keep you up all night."

"That's fine. We wanted to watch." He offered Culdesac a cup. The bobcat accepted.

Another set of thudding noises rumbled across the hills. *Bah-boom*. Closer this time. The fires stretched out farther, creating another sunset.

"We should be down there," Mort(e) said.

"No," Culdesac said. "We did our job. Let the Alphas do theirs."

"Did you get a good look at what they were doing?"

"I saw enough."

"I'd like to see a quarantine," Tiberius said. "I want do know how they do it."

"No you don't."

Their mugs filled, the three cats clinked the cups together.

"Did the humans toast with coffee?" Tiberius asked.

"Who cares?"

"Good point."

"Should we do the usual toast?" Mort(e) asked. He seemed so eager that Culdesac could not say no.

"Of course," the captain said. "To those who could not join us."

Murmur.

Luna.

Seljuk.

Nox.

The coffee scorched its way to his stomach, like ants tearing through the forest.

Mort(e) and Tiberius immediately spit their drinks into the dirt.

"Choke me, what *is* this shit?" Tiberius said.

"If you like it black, it means you're psychotic," Culdesac said, taking another sip.

"I'm perfectly sane then. Ugh, I have to wash out my cup now. Where's that wine we found?"

"It's in Logan's cave," Mort(e) said.

Tiberius left them, grumbling that he needed a drink of something that did not taste like a dog's ass.

"A dog's *ass*?" Mort(e) said.

"You could try it with sugar," Culdesac said.

"Waste of sugar," Tiberius said over his shoulder.

For Culdesac, the coffee lost all flavor. It might as well have been hot water. A general numbness crept over him, relieving his stiff joints, his aching head, his empty stomach. Something changed in him, lifting him away from this world so that he could gaze at it from afar. Nothing could hurt him. The Queen plucked him from the mud to make him more than an animal. She lifted him up once again, only this time she watched as he did it on his own. Nothing would lead him astray ever again. Nothing would silence her voice in his mind.

"Are you okay, Captain?" Mort(e) asked.

"I'm fine, I'm home."

"Did you find her?"

Culdesac turned to his Number One. The cat's face glowed orange from the distant fires.

"Sorry, sir," Mort(e) said. "I shouldn't have asked."

"I found her. But she's gone." He pointed to the smoke rising, blackening the clouds. "It's all gone."

Mort(e) nodded. "I was wondering. Do you think the Change didn't work on those people? Or did it change them in the wrong way?"

"It affects everyone differently."

"What I mean is: those people were so devoted to their old masters. The Change made us smarter. But maybe it also enhanced our capacity to love. For better or worse, I suppose."

Mort(e) had a point. But Culdesac didn't like it. "I don't think so," he said. Mort(e) was smart enough to drop it. Before long, the housecat excused himself, probably to seek a more fruitful conversation with Tiberius over a glass of wine.

Under a purple void, with the hills blackening to shadows all around him, Culdesac sat on the crate and watched the flames devour the forest. The cup grew cold in his hands, and still he stared, until his eyes grew dry and the wind carried the hint of smoke. Another enemy outpost destroyed, although—in typical human fashion—it took part of the natural landscape with it. The thudding noises quieted, reduced to a few random gunshots and tank volleys. On the horizon, an orange explosion blossomed so bright that it lit up the surrounding forest. Culdesac could see the texture of the leaves. A few of the trees collapsed, launching embers like newborn stars. The past—his past, the last remnants of the person he used to be—finally burned away, charred to ash, scraped clean from the earth to make way for new stalks to burst from the soil. In time, it would be as if the old forest had never been there.

When the sun rose again, he would lead the Red Sphinx into the west. Into the future that the Queen promised them.

Continue reading for a preview of *D'Arc*,
coming in 2017 from Soho Press.

CHAPTER ONE
THE STORY OF TAALIK

HEN THE DARKNESS passed over the water, Taalik dreamt of the temple again. A temple far beyond the seas, ruled by an ancient queen who went to war with a race of monsters. In the dream, Taalik washed ashore on a beach at nighttime. A mere fish, unable to breathe, he slapped his tail on the sharp rocks until he felt the scales cracking. His fins strained as he tried to return to the water. His lidless eye froze stiff in its socket. And then, he rose from the sand on newly formed limbs, like a crab. The claws sprouted underneath him. He opened his mouth and splayed out his gills, and the air passed through. He did not fear the light and the wind. He did not scramble back to the lapping waves, to the muted blue haze where he was born. Instead, he stood upright, no longer weightless but still strong, defying the gravity that pulled his body to the earth. He marched toward the temple—a giant mound of dirt crawling with strange creatures, each with six legs, heavily armored bodies, mouths like the claws of a lobster. Soldiers bred for killing. They worked in unison, moving as Taalik's people did, many individuals forming a whole. The creatures stood in rows on each side of him. Their antennae grazed him as he walked by, inspecting his scales, his fins. His body continued to change with each step he took. The soldiers admired his new shape, with his segmented legs, and a flexible shell that protected his spine, and tentacles that reached out from underneath, four new arms that could grasp or crush. Here, he was no mere animal, but something more, something his people would worship, something his enemies would learn to fear.

Inside the temple, he found the Queen surrounded by her children. He waited for her to speak, and soon realized that she did not have to. He understood the message ever since that first dream, and for every dream that followed. Taalik would rule, as the Queen did. There would be a new era of peace to wash away the millennia of bloodshed. No longer would his people slip into the depths of Cold Trench while watching out for predators. No longer would they see their children snatched away. They would learn, and adapt. Others would join them. Those who did not would perish. Soon, the deep would no longer hold the children of Taalik. His people would rise from the water and find new worlds to conquer.

Or, they would die. The Queen made him understand the starkness of it. There would be no circles of life anymore. Instead, there would be one current through the dark water, leading to conquest or extinction. Life or death. And to secure life, they would not run. They would have to kill.

TAALIK KEPT HIS eyes closed as he listened for the Queen's voice rumbling through the water. Orak, his Prime, floated next to him. Ever since the first revelation, she knew to leave him alone at times like this. The Queen spoke to him only when she wanted to. Even after he opened his eyes and drifted there, Orak waited. The others hovered behind her. They followed her lead. She was the first to convert, the first to mate with Taalik, the first to follow the current with him. Orak kept the others in line, reminding them of their place, but attending to their needs as well, helping to protect the eggs and rear the hatchlings. She enforced Taalik's orders, even when they went against her counsel. Taalik owed her his life. All the Sarcops did.

Taalik and his people waited under the Lip, the vein of rock that jutted out into Cold Trench, offering shelter from the predators who swam above. This refuge would not hold forever. Their enemies searched for them, driven mad with fear of this new species. Taalik tried to make peace, even ceding territory to those who claimed it as their own. But some creatures, the sharks and other bony fish, would not relent. They would never hear the Queen's song. They would never accept that the world began, rather than ended, at the surface.

Does she speak to you today, my Egg? Orak asked.

He left her waiting too long. Even Orak's enormous patience had limits, especially with the family huddled under the Lip, the food running out. A fight had broken out the day before. Orak punished the unruly ones by ordering the soldiers to feed on their eggs. They had already uprooted the nurseries and hauled them to this desolate place. Feeding on the unborn would lighten the load, and strengthen the ones bred for war.

The Queen is silent this day, my Prime, Taalik said.

A shudder in the water. Taalik gazed into the slit above, where the Lip extended across this narrow stretch of Cold Trench. In the sliver of light he saw them, the fleet of sharks, white bellied, tails waving in unison. At the lead, fatter than the others, was the one Taalik called Graydeath. He recognized the freshly healed gash on the shark's belly, courtesy of Taalik's claw. Graydeath managed to bite it off in their last encounter. The darkness passed over the water forty times before the limb fully regenerated. The other Sarcops watched the healing in amazement, and declared that no one, not even the ocean's greatest shark, could kill the Queen's chosen one.

They smell us, Orak said.

We smell them, Taalik replied.

No enemy had ever penetrated this far into their territory, least of all an army of sharks on patrol. An act of war. It meant that the scouts Taalik dispatched had most likely been killed. He ordered them to map the shoreline, and to find all of the shallows where his people would have the advantage. But the scouts also served as bait, drawing attention away from the Sarcops as they moved their young ones under the Lip. *They die for us, my Egg*, Orak told him later. *Now we live for them*.

Taalik watched the fleet passing overhead. He waited for the procession to end. It did not. It *would* not. Sharks of every breed crossed his line of sight, as thick as a bed of eels in some places. Mouths began where rear fins ended. In their rage, these solitary creatures banded together to fight a common enemy. The sharks baited him. They wanted the Sarcops to emerge and attack from the rear so that they could swoop around, encircle the strongest ones, and then descend upon the nest to destroy the eggs. Taalik saw it unfold before him, a vision planted by the Queen herself: Cold Trench clouded with blood. The torn membranes of eggs carried away by the current. Graydeath devouring the younglings while his followers waited for him to finish, not daring interrupt his victory meal lest they join it.

Summon the Juggernauts, Taalik said.

Orak emitted a clicking sound, followed by three chirps—the signal that alerted the soldier caste. The Juggernauts formed their phalanx, with Orak as the tip of the spear.

Every year, when they hibernated, the Sarcops dreamt of the Queen and her empire. And when they awoke, the Queen bestowed upon them new gifts. A language. A philosophy. Until then, their entire existence as a school of fish revolved around fear. Fear of others, of both darkness and light, of the unknown.

After the Queen's revelation, and the miracles that followed, a calm determination set in. The Sarcops would not merely react to the environment. They would reshape it as they pleased. Soon their bodies changed along with their minds, as they did in Taalik's dream. First, they sprouted limbs. Then their armored plating, making them resemble the Queen's ferocious daughters. Their mouths and throats changed. Before long, the sounds they could make matched all the images and words in their rapidly evolving brains. And then, slithering from their backs, a row of tentacles that allowed them to manipulate the world around them. Only the most loyal Sarcops advanced far enough to earn the distinction of Juggernaut alongside Taalik. The rest changed in other ways: their senses improved, their teeth sharpened, their fins became weapons. The agile Shoots could swarm their prey. The slender Redmouths could bite into their opponent and twist their bodies, pulling away flesh and bone in a whirlpool of blood. The crablike Spikes could mimic the ocean floor, setting a trap for enemies who strayed too close. Though the Juggernauts formed the vanguard, all the Sarcops knew how to fight. All would have the chance to prove themselves worthy.

Taalik told his troops that they would follow him under the Lip at full speed. They would overtake the fleet at the northern end of the crevasse, near the water's edge. There, Taalik would kill Graydeath in front of everyone. No more hiding. Today their enemies would learn what the Sarcops could do.

Taalik called for Zirsk and Asha, his third and seventh mates, who carried eggs in their pouches. When he confronted Graydeath, these two would release their eggs. Doing so would distract the sharks, who saw only the food in front of their faces. Orak watched them closely as they listened, ready to pounce on any sign of disapproval. This proved unnecessary, for Taalik's mates agreed. As a consolation for their pending sacrifice, Taalik assured them that they would recover some of the young. *We will cut them from the bellies of dead sharks,* he said. *The young ones will have a story to tell.*

Taalik twisted away from his soldiers and headed north, using the rocky Lip for cover while keeping an eye on the movement above. He felt Orak's presence, slightly behind him. She could lead if he died. But he would live. The Queen still had so much to show him.

Cold Trench grew shallower. The cover of the Lip gave way to open water, where the sharks blotted out the light piercing the surface. Taalik ascended, faster than the others, homing in on Graydeath. He felt so tiny in the expanse. The ground rising behind him blocked any hope for escape.

The water shivered as the sharks sensed movement. Graydeath aimed his snout at the intruder. His mouth split in half, a red pit of jagged teeth. Scars from numerous battles left deep divots in his skin. A severed claw still punctured his dorsal fin, a permanent reminder of some creature that died trying to fight the sharks.

Taalik charged at him, claws unsheathed, tentacles reaching out. They collided, a sound like boulders tumbling into the trench. Taalik wedged the jaw open. Tumbling and twisting, Graydeath pulled free from Taalik's grip and clamped his teeth at the root of one of his tentacles. Only by holding onto the mouth could Taalik keep the shark from shearing off the limb at the base. Blood leaked from the puncture wounds, driving Graydeath to a new realm of delirium. Taalik tried to pluck out the eye, but Graydeath squirmed his face out of reach, using his mouth as a shield. The shark's momentum dragged Taalik away from the battle, away from Cold Trench, and toward the shallows where Taalik would not be able to escape.

Taalik let him do it. Graydeath, sensing victory, thrashed again, letting go of the wounded tentacle and twisting his snout toward Taalik's head. Taalik jammed his tentacles into both gills. He could see the suckers poking into the shark's mouth. With his claws, he held the jaw open, gripping so tightly that some of the teeth broke off like old seashells. He pulled the shark toward land, toward the edge of the known world. They crashed onto a bed of rocks, kicking up dust and debris. A primitive creature, Graydeath nevertheless sensed the violation of the natural order that awaited him at the surface. Desperate, he tried to buck free of his opponent. A wave caught them, slamming them into the earth. From here, Taalik could stand. And when he did, he broke free of the water. And even with the monster still trying to tear his head off, Taalik saw the new world, the land of the Queen: a golden patch of fine sand stretching from one end to the other, anchoring a blue dome.

He held his breath as he dragged the shark out of the foamy waves. Taalik's body grew heavy, as if a giant claw tried to press him under the water where he belonged. The shark's eyes shimmered under the piercing light, stunned at the impossibility of it all. The Queen called everyone to this place, though only a few would prove worthy. Graydeath, a king of the deep, writhed in agony. No water would rush through his gills ever again. His enormous eye caked in sand, the shark trembled as life finally seeped out of his body.

Taalik felt as though he would burst. Unable to resist any longer, he opened his mouth, allowing the gills to flare out. Water sprayed from the two openings. The strange, weightless fluid of this place flowed through him, expanding his chest and rounding his segmented back. He let it out with a choking cough. Inhaling again, deeper this time, he felt the power of it. And then he let out a roar that rattled his entire body. His voice sounded so different here, higher pitched and free to skitter away in the wind. There were no waves to muffle him. He screamed his name to announce his arrival, to shake the earth so that even the Queen, in her fortress, would hear.

This shark that lay at his feet did not have a name, save for the one Taalik gave to it. Graydeath did not even understand the concept of a word, how it could rumble from the throat, and swim through the water, or float in the air, before finding purchase in someone else's mind. The Queen showed Taalik how to do this, in his dreams and now while he was awake.

Taalik gripped the bulging eyeball of the shark and wrenched it free of its socket. He held it aloft and said his name again and again until the blood dripped down his claw.

TAALIK TOWED GRAYDEATH to the site of the battle, where the Juggernauts overwhelmed the few sharks who remained. As Taalik expected, most of them fled when their leader disappeared. Warriors on both sides halted when they saw Graydeath with his jaw gaping, the lifeless fins flapping in the current. Detecting the scent of blood and defeat, the sharks retreated, leaving behind wounded comrades and severed body parts. Taalik immersed himself in the smell of it, the taste of it. The Juggernauts swam in great loops around him in a show of reverence as he placed Graydeath's corpse on the ocean floor.

Orak rushed to him and immediately went about inspecting Taalik's wounds, a faithful Prime to the end. She nudged him, forcing him to rest on the ground while she licked the gashes at the base of his tentacle, keeping them free of pathogens so they could heal. Taalik knew not to argue with her. His fourth mate, Nong-wa, attended to Orak's injury, a bite mark near her left pectoral fin. The three of them watched as the others killed the stragglers from the fleet. Zirsk and Asha ordered the Juggernauts to slice open their bellies. As Taalik promised, some of them released the eggs they had swallowed. After inspecting them, Zirsk and Asha claimed the eggs they knew to be theirs. Two competing piles formed. The others cheered them on, clicking and chirping each time they ripped open a shark. Sometimes, the fish would try to swallow the eggs again as the Sarcops extracted them, unaware that they died in the process.

Nong-wa, help with the eggs, Orak said.

Nong-wa got in a few more licks before swimming over to the others.

Taalik, the First of Us, Orak said. *I was afraid you would not return.*

I was afraid I would not find you when I did.

These fish cannot kill me.

No, Taalik said.

A shark split open, but yielded no stolen eggs, only a small, undigested fish. The Shoots devoured both.

I must tell you something, Taalik said. *I fear the others are not ready to hear.*

What is it, my Egg?

I pulled that shark above the waves. The place we cannot go, from which none return.

Orak stopped licking for a second. *And yet you returned.*

Yes. The shark died. I lived.

Taalik described the enormous weight pinning him down, the thin, tasteless air that he nevertheless could breathe. He talked about the color, the brightness of it. *The Queen chose me to break this barrier,* he said. *The place above the sea holds our destiny.*

Lead us there.

We are not ready. Too many would have to be left behind.

That has not stopped us before. He knew she meant the gambit with the eggs.

There is something else, he said. He extended his claw and held out a shiny object. She reached for it with her tentacle.

What is it? she asked.

I do not know. I pulled it from the shark's fin.

She rubbed her tentacle along the curve of the object, and then gently tapped the sharp end. *A tooth? A claw, perhaps?*

No. It is some kind of weapon, fashioned from the earth somehow. From the rock.

Who made it?

The monsters from my dream. Enemies of the Queen. They live above the surface. They tortured the shark, and his people. I saw the scars on his hide.

They are at war with the sharks, just like us.

They are at war with everyone, Taalik said. *They are more dangerous than the sharks. When the darkness passes over, I see millions of us, piled in the dirt, drying out under the sun. These monsters have hunted us for years. Destroyed our home-lands. They hate us as much as they hate her. Many of us will die if we proceed.*

Orak returned the object to Taalik. *Then we die, she said.*

She swam around to face him. Behind her, the Juggernauts held another shark while Zirsk ripped him from his gills to his rear fin. *You are the First of Us*, Orak said. *You gave us meaning and hope. But you cannot take it away. You cannot tell us what to do with it now. You gave us a choice, and we have chosen to follow you.*

She continued licking his wounds, ignoring her own injury, as was her way. He wrapped a tentacle around hers, twisting several times until the suckers latched onto one another.

They would have to abandon Cold Trench, he told her. They would not survive another hibernation period, when their enemies were sure to strike. So the Sarcops would move north, following the magnetic beacon at the pole. With luck, they would find a safe haven in the ice.

By then, Zirsk and Asha nursed their respective stacks of eggs. Shoots and Redmouths tugged on the corpses of their prisoners until some of the sharks split in two. Taalik observed in silence. Tomorrow, he would point them toward their future.